The Demise of

Alexis Vancamp 2

The Demise of
Alexis Vancamp 2

Karen Williams

www.urbanbooks.net

Urban Books, LLC
300 Farmingdale Road, NY-Route 109
Farmingdale, NY 11735

The Demise of Alexis Vancamp 2

ISBN 13: 978-1-64556-084-5
ISBN 10: 1-64556-084-8

First Mass Market Printing October 2020
First Trade Paperback Printing June 2019
Printed in the United States of America

10 9 8 7 6 5 4 3 2 1

Distributed by Kensington Publishing Corp.
Submit Orders to:
Customer Service
400 Hahn Road
Westminster, MD 21157-4627
Phone: 1-800-733-3000
Fax: 1-800-659-2436

Chapter 1

January 3, 2017

I heard the iron gate slam shut behind me. It was the last time I would hear that oppressive sound. For the past five years, I had called this place home, but now I was standing on the other side of the barbed wire–lined wall. I took a deep breath. The air smelled fresher on this side. Inside, the air was stale with desperation and hopelessness. Even in the yard the air never smelled right to me. I stretched my arms out to my side and arched my back. The sky was brighter. I saw a bird fly over my head and watched it fly out of sight. I smiled. Five years ago, a bird flying over my head signified that it would always be what I wasn't: free. Now it signified the fact that I was just as free as the damn bird. I had a new lease on life.

There's nothing to do in prison but think, and five years locked up gave me plenty of time to do just that. No matter what I was thinking about, my mind would always wander back to Santana. He was the reason I had ended up in prison. My life can be broken up into two sections: before Santana and after Santana. I don't think I will ever feel as free as I had felt before I met Santana. I had everything a woman could have wanted, hoped, or dreamed for: a handsome fiancé in medical school, a solid career with no risk of ever losing it because my dad was my boss, economic stability, an Infiniti car, my own place, friends, and great family. I had a bright future. That was taken away from me the moment I allowed Santana to *dickmitize* me. Stupid, stupid I was.

"Baby! I'm here."

I smiled as my mom ran toward me with her arms outstretched. We squeezed each other tight. It was the first time in five years we didn't have a corrections officer breathing down our necks while we hugged. I didn't want to let go.

When we finally separated, I said, "I missed you. How are you, Mom?"

She cupped my face in both her hands and stared at me almost as if in disbelief. Tears streamed down her face. She touched the long scar across my neck, a souvenir from my time behind bars. It was a permanent reminder of the awful hell of prison. Knowing that scar was there made me appreciate that I still had a voice and should savor every moment I could sing. I placed a hand over hers.

"Aww, don't cry, Mom."

She waved a hand at me and wiped her face. "I can't help it! I never thought I'd see you outside of these walls."

I wasn't sure I'd ever see her outside of the prison either. My release was a bit surprising. My sentence was twenty to life, and here I was, getting released after five. Miraculously the appeal we had filed was approved, and my charges were reduced. I thought I was dreaming as I sat in the courtroom that day. My lawyer had presented a great case on appeal and convinced the judge that it wasn't premeditated murder and it should only be considered involuntary manslaughter. It took about a week for it to sink in that I would be getting out early. After everything I had done, I thought for sure karma was going to come back and bite me. I kept waiting to wake up from my dream or to have my lawyer tell me that the judge was only joking or he had changed his mind. But it was real, and the proof was right behind me in the form of a massive brick wall and threatening iron gate. I was standing on the freedom side of that wall.

I looked at my mother, then back at the prison.

"Looks like it's just hitting you too," she said.

I chuckled and wiped a tear from my cheek. "Yeah."

"Come on. Let's go home." She grabbed my hand.

We got in my mother's car, and I got settled in the passenger's seat. She pulled away from the prison, and I reflected on the past five years. I'd always thought prison was terrible and heard stories about the horrors of life behind bars, but twenty-four years of life didn't prepare me for what I went through in there. My introduction to prison life was guards beating my ass into submission. Once word got out in the yard that the new bitch got tightened up, it was a free-for-all against me. Soon after, I was raped by a few guards, then a couple of the female inmates took their turn and forced me to lick pussy and ass. I was getting my ass beat on the regular, until I decided to take matters into my own hands. I began standing up to my bullies, and after countless black eyes and busted lips, I learned how to fight back. I went from someone who sold nothing but woof tickets, threw rock with force, and ran, to a woman who could defend herself and win fights.

Deep down, while the beatings were taking place, I knew it wasn't just because I was new and needed to prove myself. It was my own karma for the messed-up things I had done to people. People just couldn't get with how self-absorbed I was, how everything was always about me, me, me. I had it so good and hadn't dealt with any real struggle my whole life, yet there I was, locked up for fucked-up choices that hadn't needed to be made.

As I looked back on my time in prison, I realized I learned to look at myself, recognize my faults, and change. I learned not to dwell on what I conquered, and in the same vein, what I failed at. It was the past. There wasn't much need to give it any further thought. Prison, in so many respects, matured me and made me better.

So, as my mom drove and the institution became smaller and disappeared behind me, I looked ahead, and my mission became bigger.

Chapter 2

My mother's house seemed like a mirage as we pulled up. She had been filling me in on the gossip in the neighborhood—who'd moved out and who'd moved in, who got divorced, and who died. I was half listening while I got used to the fact that I wasn't pinned behind bars. Seeing the outside world was a strange experience. It looked the same but different. There were many businesses that had shuttered, and new ones had opened. But after my experience in prison, I'd look at the world with a different perspective. People were zombies and didn't understand what life was about. I still felt like I was figuring life out, but I had a better understanding than all the "free" people on the outside.

We walked into the house, and sitting on the couch was my best friend Arianna. She jumped out of her seat the moment I walked through the door.

"Ooooh, girl! Out my way! That's my best friend." She rushed me and wrapped her arms around me. We squeezed each other as if we wanted to crush one another.

"I can't believe you're home," Arianna whispered in my ear.

"I can't believe it either," I answered.

We pulled apart and held each other's hands. I looked at her beautiful face and cried. She had been a loyal friend while I was in prison. She came to visit every month I was locked up. She kept me connected to the outside world, made me feel like I still had a life. During her visits, she would share every detail of her life. She even let me be involved in her wedding planning, being so kind as to let me give advice on color schemes. I was so proud when she brought photos of her beautiful day. She was a gorgeous bride.

I still remember the day she told me she was pregnant with twin boys. We were sitting in the prison visiting room and as we talked, I could see that she was distracted. She was forgetting what she was talking about, and when I would say something, she was nodding along even when a nod wasn't called for. I finally asked her what was up.

"I'm pregnant," she said. "Twin boys."

I damn near jumped out my seat I was so excited for her. She said she was nervous to tell me because I was in lockup, and she wasn't sure how I was going to react. I was honored because I was the first of her friends she had shared her news with.

The rest of the visit, we went back and forth with baby names. Even though I wanted her to use the names I liked, I told her it was her decision because those boys would be stuck with their names for the rest of their lives, so she shouldn't go too exotic. Keep it classy, I said. When she told me she was naming one of her boys Alex after me, I damn near had a heart attack. When I got back to my cell, I became depressed. I cried deep, soul-crushing sobs. Arianna was out there having a life, while I was stuck inside for being stupid and selfish.

"Where are the boys? I asked.

"I wanted to bring them, but they are spending the weekend with their grandparents. And they don't play when it comes to spending time with their grandkids," she said, chuckling. "But I was hoping sometime this week you could stop by and meet Alex, Ashlynn, and Jabari officially."

I hadn't met her husband, Jabari, or her sons. She had never brought them to the prison to visit. She didn't want the boys to be exposed to the system and be around the energy of a prison, and Jabari was more than happy to stay home with them because he didn't do institutions because of his job, which I understood. He was a supervising prosecutor for the county.

I was lucky to still have my bestie after everything I had done. She made it so comfortable for me to be back home. I wished I could go back to the days when we would cut it up at my father's house and laugh like hyenas, but I knew we were way beyond that. Too much had taken place, and I had done too much damage to ever be able to get back to the way it was. It was a new relationship between me and everyone. I was grateful to have a second chance. I would live with the guilt of how I had treated Arianna for the rest of my life.

"Come on, you two. The food is ready," my mother said from the kitchen.

"Mom! You didn't have to do all of this," I said when I entered the kitchen and saw the amount of food she had prepared. "When did you have time to make all of this?"

"I wanted to make my baby's homecoming special," she said.

She had made pizza, chili cheese fries, tacos, chips and guacamole, fried pork chops, fried chicken and waffles, macaroni and cheese, buttery biscuits, mashed potatoes and fried cabbage, bacon grilled cheese sandwiches, ribeye steaks, and a freaking crab boil with crawfish, shrimp, sausage, and lobster. It was a mish-mash of all my favorite foods.

I laughed and grabbed a plate. I started with the chicken and waffles. It was better than Roscoe's, and I thought nothing could be better than that. I made a mental note to visit Roscoe's as soon as possible. Man, I missed that place. Arianna piled mac and cheese, pork chops, and biscuits onto hers.

My mom sat across from us and watched me eat with a silly smile on her face.

"What?" I asked.

"I'm just so happy to have my baby back home," she said. "Your hair grew back so long and pretty."

I nodded before biting into the chicken. I closed my eyes, savoring the flavor. Prison food was awful. This was the first time in five years I'd had a homecooked meal, and it was delectable.

My mom chuckled.

After chewing and swallowing, I said, "Yep, it did."

"You had no more problems with it?"

"To be honest, I wasn't having problems with my hair like I told you. I had to cut it because it was putting me at a disadvantage."

"What do you mean?" my mom asked.

"When I first started getting in prison fights, the other chicks would go straight for the hair pull. I needed to cut it to give me a chance."

"Prison fights?" Arianna said.

"Alexis, why didn't you tell us?" my mom asked, tears in her eyes.

"I didn't want to worry anyone. It was my burden to bear. Don't worry now. I'm out and never going back."

"Of course I'm worried. I'm your mother."

"And I'm your best friend," Arianna added. "Now, tell us how you beat ass in prison."

I laughed. "Oh, stop."

"Serious, girl. I wanna hear some realness from behind bars," Arianna said.

I rolled my eyes. "You crazy, but okay," I said. "I had come back to my cell after getting beat on the yard by three bitches who had targeted me right from jump. This one fat lesbian, Whosie, decided she didn't like me and made it her mission to torture me. Personally, I think she was attracted to me and wanted to make me her bitch. Anyway, she and two other bitches jumped me on the yard. I came back to my cell lookin' a mess. My cellie, Cashmere, was laying in her bunk. She was a bad bitch, so she had the bottom bunk with no argument from me. You know what I'm sayin'? So, Cashmere says to me 'If you don't fight back, you're in for a long, miserable life in here.' 'I know,' I said. 'I'm fightin' back, but I can't take on three at once.'

"Cashmere wasn't having it. She got out of her bunk, went into her locker, and took out electric clippers. She wasn't allowed to have them, but she had pull with the guards, so they looked the other way when it came to Cashmere. She took the clippers, had me stand over our sink, and began to shave my head. I started to protest, but Cashmere overpowered me. To be honest, I didn't protest too much, especially when I saw myself in the mirror. Shaving my head did something to me. I felt like an African warrior.

"Cashmere said, 'Tomorrow on the yard, I'll handle the other two. It's time for you to take care of Whosie's ass. She won't know what to do if she can't pull your hair. It's the only way that fat bitch can win a fight.' The next day, Cashmere and I stepped up to Whosie and her girls. Before anyone said a word, I swung on Whosie and clocked her in her jaw. She reached for my head but had nothing to grab. I easily avoided her and started going ham on her. Cashmere didn't have to do anything because the other two were so stunned they didn't fight. It was the last time anyone fucked with me."

"You bad ass, girl," Arianna said.

My mother looked stunned.

"You okay there?" I asked.

"I just hate to think of you having to survive like that," she said.

"It was my own fault I was in there."

To tell the truth, I really didn't want to talk about prison. I wanted to put it behind me. Thoughts of prison brought me back to thoughts of Santana and the piss-poor decisions I made because of him. I was naïve, stupid, and selfish. The way I had treated people was inexcusable, and it was all because of a man I had no business dealing with. Back then, I didn't give a shit. But after five years in the pen, I sure did.

My mother looked over my shoulder to something behind me. Her face turned from concern to elation. I turned around to see my sister with her husband. They stood in the doorway of the kitchen, my sister's husband holding a baby girl.

I let out a squeal, dropped the chicken wing on my plate, and stood from the table. It had been five years since I'd seen my sister. I would write her and send her cards every holiday, congratulating her on milestones in her life, the most important being her wedding and the birth of her daughter. She never responded, but that was okay. I didn't hold any ill will toward her. Not at all. My goal at this point would be trying to establish a relationship with her because, truthfully, we'd never really had one.

I went to embrace my sister first. She took a step back to block me. There was a coldness in her eyes. Embarrassed, I backed up a little, nodded, and smiled.

"Hello, Bria."

She looked away without acknowledging me. I'd always thought my sister was pretty, but she had grown into a very beautiful woman. Her slim figure was fuller, less young girl and more mature woman. I attributed that to the baby weight. Her face was a little rounder, and her skin was clear. Looking at her, you would never know she had battled a drug addiction.

Her husband, Casey, who was our pastor's son and now the current pastor, embraced me and said, "Good to see you, Alexis."

In the time since I'd been away, he'd gone from a young boy following his daddy around, learning the scripture, to a grown man leading the flock. By marrying Casey, my sister became the first lady.

I reciprocated his affection, pulled away, and smiled. "Same to you, Casey." I looked at the baby in his arms.

"Is this my niece?"

He chuckled. "Yes, it is."

She was so pretty. I smiled down at her little face as her wide eyes mean-mugged me. She had a set of golden, almond-shaped eyes and incredibly chubby cheeks I just wanted to bite. How adorable she was. I forced myself to block out any bad thoughts and bask in the cuteness of the baby in front of me.

"Now, I know Mama has told me her name, but I've forgotten. What's her name?" I asked.

He took a deep breath and said, "Nya Chardonnay Royalty Summer Rain."

I saw my mom smirk.

I tried to keep my smile, but the name choice was surprising. "That is a mouthful."

"Why you think I took a breath before saying it?" He laughed. "I call her Ny,"

"Can I hold her?"

"Sure." Casey held her toward me.

My sister stepped in quickly and snatched her away. "No! I need to change her." She walked off with the baby in her arms.

My mom shook her head.

Her husband looked confused. Then his cell rang. He checked the caller ID. "Excuse me," he said and walked off.

I sat back down to continue eating. I didn't mention the awkwardness with my sister. It would be better to ignore it. There was no need to start any drama.

My sister walked back into the room with the baby. She sat down and eyed me. I pretended not to see it. Her husband reemerged and started making two plates. He sat next to her and put the plates on the table. My sister looked down at her plate, scanned the table, and screwed up her face. "Mom, why didn't you make or buy chicken fingers?"

"Because this dinner wasn't for you. It was for your sister. Now, there is plenty to choose from, and even some more food in the refrigerator that I couldn't squeeze on the table. Choose from that and hush."

She sucked her teeth and looked at her husband's plate as if nothing on his plate interested her either. "See what else is in the refrigerator," she said.

He nodded and followed her directions. "Pizza?" he asked, holding a box of cold slices. She shrugged her shoulders and rolled her eyes.

Bria was trying to eat a slice of pizza. The baby became fussy and started crying, which caused Bria to almost drop the baby. She grabbed the baby aggressively and situated her on her lap. Poor Nya started crying, but Bria ignored her and munched on the pizza. She wasn't only ignoring the baby; she was ignoring the rest of us at the table as well. The energy in the room changed drastically with Bria there. We sat there in silence, waiting for her to tend to Nya.

Finally having enough, my mom stood and walked toward with her arms open. "Give me the baby so you can eat." Once my mom had the baby in her arms, she started cooing and rocking her as the baby calmed down.

To break the tension in the room, Arianna started talking cheerfully to me. "I know there's a ton of things you want to do after you get everything settled."

"To be honest, I hadn't really thought about it. I know there are some loose ends I'd like to tie up."

"Right, but I'm sure you want to do some of the things you haven't been able to do being locked up—like the movies, the club, maybe. Even go to Burke Williams and get a deep tissue massage?" my mom said.

Out of nowhere, my sister let out a shrill scream. "Really!"

Everyone looked at her, surprised.

"Bria, what the hell is your problem?" my mom asked.

"So, we're going to just sit here and ignore the fucking pink elephant with the glitter all over it in the room?"

We all looked at her, confused.

She turned to my mother. "Mom, really? Are you going to sit here and pretend?" She shoved her plate away. "Mom! I've never known you to be fake. Until today."

"Shut your goddamn mouth, Bria!" my mother shouted.

Bria looked my way and snarled at me, "You are the reason that Daddy is dead! You! Had you not brought that filth Santana into our lives, all this shit would have never happened! Because of you, I had to go to rehab! Mom and Daddy divorced, and Daddy died because of all the stress. All because you wanted some new dick!"

"Bria!" my mom shouted, causing the baby to cry.

"I'm not happy you're home. I wish you had died in that cell instead of Daddy, Alexis! I fucking hate you, and I always fucking will!" She stood to her feet and shoved her plate to the floor. Then she took her fork and threw it at me before running from the kitchen.

Chapter 3

Two years ago, when my dad passed away, I felt ill, literally. I had been fighting a flu for three days and felt like death. The guard came to my cell and told me the warden wanted to see me. I could barely get out of bed. I shuffled my way to the warden's office, aching every step of the way. I sat in the warden's office, and she got right to why I was there.

"Your father has passed away," she said. "And because of your good standing within the prison, we will allow you to attend the funeral."

I could barely thank her. I wanted to fall asleep right there in the office.

The warden felt my forehead. "She's got a fever. Take her to the medical unit."

They gave me an IV, and I slept for two days in the medical unit. I was feeling better in time for my father's funeral.

My daddy had passed from a stroke, and I, too, wanted to die. I wanted to take his place and have him still be here. But I didn't have supernatural powers, so my father's fate couldn't be reversed no matter how much I wanted it. I was still here and my dad . . . he wasn't.

Bria had skipped my father's funeral. When I asked my mother why, she said Bria told her it was me or her. My mom didn't exclude me, so Bria excluded herself.

It sucked that my sister still hated me and felt I was responsible for his death. I mean, I won't lie; I always blamed myself and felt that the pain of his daughter being locked away for life was eating at him all the time. Of course, my mom denied it, but it was how I always felt. But I was grateful that I was able to attend his funeral and properly say goodbye to him.

I closed my eyes as I thought of her painful words again. That girl hated my guts. How would I ever be able to have a relationship with her if she felt that way about me?

"That damn girl." My mom shook her head and rocked the baby, patting her back gently.

Arianna stood from the table. "I gotta get going. Jabari and I have the house to ourselves, and we both want to take advantage of it." She winked at me.

I chuckled, stood back from the table, and followed her to the living room. "So, Alexis, how about you stop by on Wednesday? We can really hang out, and you can meet my little family?"

"Okay. Works for me."

We said our byes, and I closed the door behind her. Immediately, I felt someone shove me out of the way. When I turned around, Bria scowled at me and pushed her way out the door. I figured it was better to leave her alone. I would try again, but not today. Not while she was so angry.

"Good night," her husband said, following behind her with the baby in his arms.

"Good night," I said in a quiet voice.

I closed the door, turned around, and walked to the living room sofa. I sat down and took a deep breath. It was the first time I had been alone in five years. The sofa was the most comfortable thing I'd sat on in a long time. The soft cushions cradling my body felt luxurious. I leaned my head back and closed my eyes. Even though I was alone, I still heard the sounds of prison in my head. I wondered if they would ever leave me.

"Oh there you are," I heard my mother say. She sat next to me on the sofa. "I do hope that you are not even about to let your childish-ass sister get to you. She may have a husband and a baby, but that young woman still has not grown up."

My mother had never really talked about my father's death. Her only words were for me not to internalize it. I mean, the sentiment behind her words was nice, but still it did nothing for how much anguish I felt behind my daddy's death. Point blank period, I had been downright deceitful to my parents for Santana. I mean, I stole from him. I had been remorseful even before my dad passed, and once he died, I damn near wanted to claw my face off.

"Remember. Hindsight is twenty-twenty, baby."

I smiled at my mom because she was for sure reading my thoughts.

"Remember, you made peace with your father well before he passed, so there's no room and certainly no need to feel guilt. Now, pain I can understand, because it's what I still feel. Despite our divorce, I miss that man. I still love that man. Umph." She shook her head. She tried to hold back, but tears started falling. "He had made mistakes, but I made some as well. I've done some things in this marriage that I shouldn't have for far too long. It was almost like I set the both of us up for failure from the very beginning."

"What do you mean?" She had never spoken like that before about herself in the context of her marriage.

She paused and stared at me for a moment like she was contemplating whether she should tell me any more. Then she shook her head. "Nothing, Alexis, I just want you to understand that I feel bad too."

I grabbed one of her hands. "But, Mom, if you are telling me not to blame myself, then maybe you should take your own advice."

She nodded. "It's a little deeper than that . . . but you're right. Your dad was always stressed, Alexis. He had high blood pressure."

That's when my tears started. "But when I went away, it had to make it worse."

"Yes, it killed him inside to see his baby girl locked away, and he felt powerless to do anything to get you out. He put the burden on his heart. He blamed himself because he felt he should have made more of an effort to get you away from Santana. He just never thought it would go as far as it did. That you would have even been in the position that bastard placed you in. But regardless, *you* got to let that go. Baby, you're the last person that should feel sad. If I wasn't such a weak bitch, he wouldn't have been around, because I would have aborted him. We wouldn't been in this." She was holding one of her hands balled up into a fist in the air.

"So, baby, truth is, in more ways than one"—she lowered her fist, unballed her hand, and aimed a finger at her chest—"I blame myself for this just as much as your father blamed himself. Santana hated *me*. He wanted to hurt *me*."

I remember the day my mother told me the truth about Santana—that he was really my half-brother and the product of a simple fling that resulted in a baby. The guy was never someone she met in college like she had originally said; he was actually her dad's business partner that she carried on an affair with behind her parents' back. Although he was twenty-four years older, she said they both loved each other, and when she found out she was pregnant by him, the plan was to run away together and keep the baby. That was, until she discovered that he was also fucking her mother and playing them both. Only she didn't discover it alone. Her father also found out. My mother's mother begged her husband for forgiveness, and he did forgive her, providing my grandmother broke off the relationship, which she did.

However, my grandfather's business partner did not easily move. In fact, he didn't move on at all. What he did instead was kill both my mother's parents in cold blood. He showed up at their house, telling them he wanted to talk. My grandfather told my mother to stay hidden upstairs. He didn't want them to see each other. My mother was never sure what happened next, but she heard screaming then gunshots. She ran downstairs and saw her parents lying on the floor, surrounded by a pool of blood. The front door to their house had been left open when the business partner fled. She had nightmares of the scene for years after that.

She ended up being raised by her aunt, who forced her to give up the baby. She was seventeen. Once she turned eighteen, she escaped to college in California and never looked back. She met my father after college, but he wasn't her first choice. There was another man that had her heart in California. Her college boyfriend stayed in Northern California to begin working in Silicon Valley, but my mother felt she needed to get back south. When

she got pregnant with me, my dad did the right thing
and married her. It wasn't the incredible love story I
envisioned. She said my father always loved her, but
she had to grow to love him. I couldn't hate my mother
for that. I couldn't. As far as I was concerned, she was a
young, impressionable kid who an older man had taken
advantage of. She was the real victim.

"Baby, I know we've had this conversation countless
times, but I really want you to know—"

"Mom, yes, we have had this conversation countless
times. And if you want to have them for more, that's
fine. But you need to understand that I hold no ill will
toward you. I don't blame you, Mom. I love you like I
always have. Nothing changed that. And to be honest,
this situation with Santana—all I want to do is put it
behind me. Move forward. I can't change the past, but I
want to right all the wrong I've done to people on account
of Santana. I was selfish, foolish, and penis crazy. Well,
these five years locked up gave me no choice but to see
the raw truth of what I did, how I unapologetically hurt
people. I am lucky to be out of there. God gave me a
second chance, and I promise to right all the wrong or die
trying."

"Well, you don't need to right anything with me.
We're good, and you can stay here as long as you like. I
went out and bought you some clothes, shoes, socks, and
underwear. And your old room is ready for you."

"Thanks, Mom. I'm lucky to have you."

I thought back to the people that I did need to mend.
I couldn't see them being as understanding, but it didn't
matter. I was willing to do the work, no matter how hard
it was.

Just then, someone rang the doorbell, followed by a loud knock. My mother and I looked at each other.

"Who the hell is that?" my mom mumbled before getting up and going to the door. Once there, my mother said, "Who is it?"

"Parole! Open the door," the female yelled.

My mother's head snapped back at the tone of the person's voice. She knew I was on parole and my parole officer would be coming to see me once I got released.

I stood and rushed to the door. "Let me handle it, Mom," I said.

My mom shook her head and walked away and stood in front of the fireplace with her arms crossed under her chest.

When I unlocked and opened the door, I came face to face with a light-skin woman with freckles dotting her face. She was tall and skinny. Her braids were thrown back in a ponytail.

"Are you or does Alexis Vancamp live here?"

"Yes. That's me"

"I'm Ms. Wilkes." She flashed her badge at me with one hand and motioned for me to back up with the other. I did, and she stormed into the living room. Once I closed the door behind her, she said, "Now, who are you?"

"I'm her mother," Mom snapped.

She lifted her right brow at my mother's tone.

"Is there some sort of problem?"

I gave my mom a look, silently begging her to be quiet. But she wouldn't.

"I don't like anyone banging on my door. Aren't you supposed to let us—"

"I ain't gotta let y'all know shit. That's what an unannounced visit is. You got a problem with that, I can gladly send her punk ass back where she was."

My mother and Ms. Wilkes had a stare-down for a few seconds before my mom huffed out an impatient breath and nodded her head.

Ms. Wilkes pulled a pair of latex gloves out of her back pocket and said, "Show me where you sleep, Vancamp."

I nodded. "Mom, am I sleeping in my old room?"

"Yes, you are," Mom said. It was so soon after my release that I hadn't even had time to see the room I was sleeping in.

"Right this way." I walked up the stairs, and she followed behind me.

I opened the door and let her enter. The room was spotless. It must have taken my mother hours to get it like that. She had put all new bedding and curtains up. I swear she even painted the room.

Ms. Wilkes proceeded to destroy my clean and tidy room. She pulled all the pillows, sheets, and blankets off the bed and flipped the mattress over. She pulled open all my drawers, shoved clothes out, and pulled everything out of the closet.

I said nothing and kept a poker face. I was used to this after spending five years in prison. All this could be cleaned up.

"Any guns in the home?"

"No," I said.

She then searched the bathroom in my room, then the hallway restroom. When she approached my mother's room, she was blocked entrance by my mother.

"No. This is where I draw the line. She is on parole. I'm not. Why the hell do you have to check my room?" my mother demanded.

Ms. Wilkes placed both her hands up as if in surrender. She then handed me her business card. "Your appoint-

ment with me is tomorrow at eight, and don't be late."
With that, she paused, looked my mother up and down,
and busted up laughing. "You think you running shit, but
you not."

My mom gasped at her comment, but my look urged
her to say nothing.

Ms. Wilkes walked down the stairs and out of the
house.

As soon as she was out of earshot, my mother said,
"What a fucking bitch!"

I nodded my head and sighed before going back into
my room. I was hoping I would be able to spend my first
night home soaking in a tub and sleeping in my old room
in my old bed. That would have to wait so I could clean
up the mess she had made. I still wasn't fully out of the
system.

"I'll help you." My mom picked up a shirt off the floor
in my room.

"No, I got it. You have already done so much to help
me."

But my mom was stubborn and did not leave the room
until the mess was completely cleaned up.

I opted out of taking a bath and took a quick shower
instead. I was exhausted. The day was eventful to say
the least. It took me back to being a teenager, when I
was madly in love with Dannon, and in college, living a
charmed life with no responsibilities. Who would have
ever thought I'd end up in the situation with a booking
number? Sometimes you just never know. The important
thing was I had grown from the experience, and thank
God for second chances.

***

A loud banging on the front door woke me from a sound sleep. It sounded like someone was hitting it with a hard object. I jolted up in bed. Before I could even get a foot out of the bed, I heard a loud bang. I rushed out of my room and ran directly into my mother, as she came out of her room.

"What is going on?" she asked.

I shrugged and led the way down the stairs. Midway down, I saw a total of five sheriffs with guns drawn, entering the house through the kicked-in door. They rushed us, aiming their guns at our heads.

"Get down!"

I immediately froze on the steps and dropped to my knees with my hands up. But not my mom.

"What do you think you're doing in my house?" my mother demanded at the top of her lungs.

One of the sheriffs flung my mother onto the floor while yelling, "Are you deaf? Get the fuck down!" He placed her in handcuffs as another officer placed handcuffs on me.

"Why the fuck are you putting us in handcuffs?" my mother demanded.

"Lady, had you shut the fuck up like I said and got down when we asked, you would have not been. So, it's best you keep your mouth shut."

"Her parole officer, that evil bitch, was just here! All of this shit isn't necessary. It's four o'clock in the damn morning."

"Well, she's not here now, all right? We are, so shut the fuck up!"

"Mom, please just listen to them," I said.

My mom clamped her mouth shut.

The third sheriff said, "Which one of you is Alexis Vancamp?"

"Me," I said.

"Okay. Well, you're on parole. You should know what happens next. We have to do a search and seizure."

My mother and I were both escorted to the couch. We sat down and watched them tear up the house. They flipped over things and tore into cabinets. My mom sat there and cried. I felt terrible. It reminded me of the day the Jamaicans came and tore up my mother's house on account of the money Santana owed. I couldn't even look my mother's way. I understood the sheriffs had to do their job, but why did they have to be so vicious about it? It wasn't like this was my home. It was my mother's. But then, I put her in this position with the screwed-up mess I had pulled years ago, being foolish and chasing behind that dirty man I had no business even dealing with.

About a good thirty minutes later, they emerged, and two of the sheriffs took the cuffs off of us.

"Next time, keep your fucking mouth shut, ma'am."

I knew my mother wanted to say something else, but for my sake, she didn't.

He turned to me and said, "Don't forget to go see your parole agent at eight a.m. sharp."

I nodded and looked away.

Chapter 4

I made sure to get to the parole office early the next morning. Ms. Wilkes made me wait in the lobby for almost two hours before she came to get me. I assumed it was a punishment for my mother's attitude the night before. I wasn't going to let it affect me, though. I'd been tested and tried in prison. Waiting two hours in a warm lobby was a cake walk.

When she did get me, I was pulled into an interview room, and for a good thirty seconds she simply stared at me. I promised myself I wouldn't let her see me feeling uncomfortable, so I let her do her thing.

"So . . . how was that parole visit?"

I simply stared back at her. Was she the reason the sheriffs came to the house? If it wasn't routine, which was what I initially thought, then it was a shame she did that just to fuck with me. I could just imagine how horrible it was going to be under her supervision.

"So, I'm an evil bitch?"

I looked at her, surprised, not knowing what to say.

"Speak."

"No. I don't think so. I don't know you to say that, ma'am."

"What about your bougie-ass mammy? Does she think I'm an evil bitch?"

"No, not at all." The sheriffs must have told her my mother had said that. How else would she have known?

She stared down at me for a few seconds. I cleared my throat and looked away. When I fearfully looked her way again, she was typing at a fast pace while eying me. She then turned the screen my way. There was a paragraph on the screen that said:

On 01/04/2017, The Los Angeles Sheriff's Department arrived at 2343 Belmont Street. Long Branch CA 90805, to conduct a search and seizure check at the parole officer's discretion. The mother and the client, Alexis Vancamp, were extremely uncooperative, and as a result, we had to place them in handcuffs. As we proceeded to do our routine search, the mother shouted, "That, dumb evil bitch was just here!" No contraband was found.

My heart thudded, but I continued reading.

There is no action required at this time, but I recommend this parolee be placed under strict supervision.

I finished reading, looked away for a second, then turned back to her. "Look, I'm sorry for what my mother said, but—"

She pointed her index finger in my face, and her tongue flicked against her middle upper gums, where two teeth were missing. "Oh, it's too late for that. Nobody insults me."

I gasped.

"You need to let your mama know that like I told her, she not running shit. I will come there whenever I please and search what I please. Now, tell me this. What kind of idiot comes from the area you come from then decides to sell her pussy in a hotel room to a white man she then kills? Tell me something. Did you get off on that shit? Killing him?"

"I didn't mean for it to happen," was all I said in my defense.

"Chile, please. You are all kinds of stupid. A privileged, lazy, spoiled bitch. So fucking what if you're pretty? 'Cause pretty and dumb not a good combination."

"I made mistakes," I said, nodding. "But if it's all right with you, I would like to focus on my parole."

She smirked at me. "I don't give a shit what you like. We go by my rules, and we discuss what *I choose* to discuss." Her tongue curled in the center of her lower mouth, where there was a gap due to two more missing teeth. "As far as I'm concerned, you took a man's life, so they should have never let your ass out."

What was this about? Because I was attractive, or because I had murdered a person? I kept a poker face so she didn't see what I was thinking, because I knew I would have to deal with her. I thought about going to her supervisor, but a couple things could happen from that. The right thing would be that she would be disciplined for how she was treating me, and I could get to another parole officer that treated me better. But with my luck, I would probably get moved to an officer who would treat me worse. Another outcome would be her supervisor telling her that I reported her, and then she would treat me worse. I didn't want to take any chances. I would just have to be nice to this woman, comply with my terms of parole, and deal with her extra bullshit. It could be worse, after all. I could still be locked up, dealing with things far worse than this lady in front of me.

She threw a plastic cup at me. "Go bring me some pee."

Since I had been waiting for her for over two hours, I had already used the restroom. I told her, "I can't go right now. I used it already in the lobby."

Her head snapped back. "Ohhh, so you don't wanna test!" Her voice got really loud. She picked up the phone and said, "Let me call the sheriffs to pick you up since you're refusing to test."

Panic hit me. After getting out, I couldn't go back. Ms. Wilkes showed who she was—shady and unreasonable. I had met corrections officers like her. It made no difference to complain. Nothing ever happened except more retaliation. I would just have to be on my P's and Q's with her.

"No. I just need some water and a few minutes," I said nervously.

"Get up," she snapped.

I did, and so did she.

"Step out into the lobby. You have exactly five minutes to be ready."

It turned out that I waited another hour and a half. I drank and drank from the water fountain and waited and waited, and still, she wouldn't come out.

I went to the reception desk so they could call her three different times, and still she wouldn't come out to test me. My bladder felt like it was sitting on my lap. I was tapping a foot against the chair and trying to place my mind elsewhere, but just seeing someone take a sip of water from the fountain, the security slurping on his soda, or someone stepping out of the bathroom was agony for me. I was at the point where I felt I had no control on my vaginal muscles to hold the pee in. So, I stood carefully, saying fuck it, and took steps toward the bathroom.

That's when I heard, "What you doing?"

Before I could stop myself and control it . . . I peed on myself!

To this, Ms. Wilkes burst out in laugher so loud that the entire lobby was looking at me as piss ran down my legs and saturated my jeans. I looked down in shame.

"How does a grown woman pee-pee on herself?" she asked.

I didn't respond. I just stood there to see what her next words would be. I wanted to ignore her ass and run into the bathroom to clean myself up.

"I can't do anything with you now. Just be back here tomorrow at eight a.m., and you bet not be late. Also, if you fail to show up, I will put out a bench warrant for your arrest, Ms. Incest. Now, go fuck your brother some more."

I put my head down in shame and rushed in the restroom to clean myself up the best I could.

Once I was able to get home, shower, and change from the ordeal that happened at the parole office, I calmed down. However, from the time I walked out in embarrassment amidst the giggles and made it to my car, I cried and felt like a fool. It was obvious I was going to have nothing but problems with my parole officer. I wished to God I didn't have to deal with her, and I dreaded seeing her again, but her words came back to me: *I'll put out a bench warrant for your arrest.*

As I stepped outside my house, I tried to block it out and let it go. It made no sense harping over something that had happened and would never change. And while humiliating, yes, at the same time, I didn't know any of those people, so whatever. I focused my attention on taking a trip over to Arianna's home. She had told me she decided to stay in Long Beach, Bixby Knolls.

When I pulled up, I couldn't help but admire her home. The neatly trimmed lawn and roses placed perfectly amongst the yard were picture perfect. To top it off, a Range Rover and a Mercedes truck sat in the driveway.

I walked up the steps. There were two rocking chairs and a porch swing on the porch. A sign just above the doorbell read: THE MARSHALLS.

I smiled and rang the doorbell as I wiped my feet on the WELCOME HOME mat.

A very striking man answered the door. He was tall, with broad shoulders. His skin was the shade of peanut butter, and he had a chiseled jawbone. If I had to say he favored a celebrity, I would say he looked like Cam Newton.

He smiled and said, "Alexis?"

"Yes. Hi." I held one of my hands out for him to shake.

"Girl, if you don't stop. We're family now." He pulled me in his arms for a bear hug.

I laughed and embraced him as best I could, which wasn't easy because he was so tall and his chest was huge. Jesus. Arianna had hit the jackpot.

He pulled away and stepped back so I could enter. "Come on in."

I stepped inside.

"Is that Alexis?" I heard a female voice say.

"Yes, babe."

"Tell her I'll be right out."

"Have a seat," he said.

I was surprised he was so nice to me. I almost expected to get a side-eye for being the screwup that I was.

I stared around the home, which was really nice. It was all indicative of her personality. It was spacious and decorative, with fluffy couches and tons of pillows. Distinctive art hung on the walls, along with countless family pics. I stared at her wedding pictures and pics of her twins when they were first born.

Wow, I thought. *I missed all those moments.*

"Would you like something to drink?"

"No, thank you," I said.

Suddenly, an adorable little boy with sandy-colored hair came running into the living room and stood in front of me. Arianna came out next with another little boy she was holding in her arms.

Jabari grabbed the little boy and swung him in his arms, showering him with kisses. The little boy started giggling. He put the little boy down and told him, "Alex, say hi to Alexis."

The little boy walked up to me and threw himself in my arms.

"Awww. Thank you," I said as his little arms wrapped around me.

"And this is Ashlynn. But,"—she lowered her voice and pointed to the boy in her arms— "this one here is a little anti-social. Watch."

"Ashlynn. Say hi to my friend Alexis."

Ashlynn turned his little head my way and turned back around, shouting, "No!"

I laughed.

Both Arianna and Jabari said sorry at the same time.

"No, it's fine."

Jabari kissed Alex on one of his chubby little cheeks and walked up to Arianna. He whispered something in her ear that made her blush and shove him with her free arm. He then kissed Ashlynn before saying, "Alexis, I wish I could stay and chat it up with you and my wife, but I have to tie up some loose ends that my staff just can't do without me. Sorry." He leaned over and kissed me on my right cheek before heading out.

"No problem. I'm sure we will have more opportunities to catch up."

"Bye, babe," Arianna said. She watched him walk out of the room.

She turned back to me. "Come on. I'll show you a quick tour of our home."

I followed behind her and little Alex. It was a spacious yet cozy house. Her boys shared a bedroom that was just too adorable and decorated with dinosaurs. She said her boys were obsessed with them. She even had a play room with dozens and dozens of toys. There was a family room and the notorious "do not enter room" that was completely white. Her kitchen, I noted, was also huge.

"This is such a big kitchen," I exclaimed.

"Girl, Jabari would have a fit if he didn't come home to a home-cooked meal. So, the compromise was that I get a big kitchen." She giggled.

We settled outside in her backyard that looked like a miniature park. Her kids ran around as soon as the double doors that led from the dining room to the backyard opened. She had a huge swing set, a tree house, a sandbox, and ride-on cars everywhere. The setup was exactly what I would want if I had a husband and kids. Arianna and I sat on the deck and watched them play.

When they both fought over a scooter, Arianna said calmly, "Boys, play nice and share." Ashlynn gave it to Alex, and he scooted away, giggling.

Arianna then sighed deeply before smiling. "They are a handful, but I sure love my boys."

"So, how does it feel, Mom?" I felt silly for asking her this, because I had asked her before, but I didn't know what else to say.

"Well, I must say that it is indeed a lot, having two munchkins to run after all day. But I love it, Alexis. I wouldn't trade this for anything, I swear to you."

My eyes moistened with tears that threatened to spill. I quickly recovered by coughing and closing my eyes for a few seconds. I knew why I had gotten emotional. I was ecstatic for my friend, but also, I couldn't help but think that this was the life Dannon and I were supposed to live if I hadn't screwed up. We would be married, living in a beautiful home with kids. But me . . . I messed that up. I looked down at my hands regretfully.

"You okay?"

"Yes. I'm fine. Do you want more?"

Her brows furrowed, deep in thought. "Well, I'm not sure." She looked sad for a moment. "I had always hoped we could have carried our kids together. I used to envision throwing baby showers and being in each other's weddings. Then when they said you were never getting out, I gave up on that." She clapped her hands together. "But now there is hope!"

Confused, I asked, "Hope?"

"Yes! You're home. There is a chance for you to find love again, get married, and have kids."

Have kids. I closed my eyes briefly as memories flooded back to me.

About two months after the trial, once I had settled into the prison, I felt it. Something was off. Really, really off. It was not the need to sleep all the time, not the back pain. I attributed that to my depression for fucking up my life. What caused my concern was that I was feeling dizzy as hell. I explained it to the corrections officer on my tier, and she brushed it off, told me to stop being a baby and to get back in my cell. In my third month in prison, I blacked out as I stepped out of my cell for dinner. They rushed me to the infirmary to determine what was wrong. I was told quite simply, "You're pregnant." But I was not just pregnant; I was eighteen weeks pregnant! And well, we know who the father was. Santana.

When I heard the news, I buried my face in my hands. I could not have a baby in prison. I was never getting out. What kind of life would that provide for a baby? What would happen to him or her? Would they allow my mother to raise the baby? And knowing I would never get out, that baby would have to see me behind bars. It was guaranteed that the baby would hate me for ruining their life and depriving them of a real mother and a healthy, normal upbringing.

And that was the least of my worry. I was pregnant with my brother's child. I definitely couldn't go through with the birth. I had learned long ago having a baby with a sibling can cause mutations and abnormalities. The baby could have immune disorders, mental health problems, and there was even a chance I could affect that baby's chance of having kids. And what about the public humiliation the child would have to bear living in a world where their parents were blood related? No, I couldn't bring that baby into the world. I just couldn't!

The decision to get an abortion made me immediately regret all the times I had judged other women and young girls for terminating their pregnancies. So, when the doctor asked me, "What would you like to do?" I didn't hesitate to tell him I wanted an abortion.

"The longer we wait, the higher the risk. We need to get you in as soon as possible. I'll speak with the warden."

A few days later, just as my belly was rounding, I was transported to an outside clinic in Downey to have the procedure done. When we arrived, there were anti-abortion protesters standing in front of the clinic. Some were holding posters that showed horrible pictures of tiny babies all bloodied, and some had pictures where babies were mutilated. Their presence didn't make it any easier. I hated all of them. They had no right to shame me for the decisions I was making on my behalf. They didn't know my situation. I tried to ignore all of it and reminded myself why I was doing what I was doing. I could not bring a baby into the world by my brother.

I was escorted to the entrance by two prison guards. A man wearing a pair of blood-stained scrubs followed us and continued making swift motions like he was scooping something out of his abdomen with a scalpel. I was afraid he was going to shank me with the scalpel. I closed my eyes and allowed the guards to usher me into safety. Once inside, I was taken to a back room, where a female nurse was waiting.

The two officers stood by the door while the nurse, an elderly blond woman with glasses, handed me a clipboard and instructed me to fill out the forms. I did so quickly and handed it back to her.

She scanned the forms and then told me. "You know you have other options. You do not have to terminate your pregnancy if you do not want to. Even though you are detained, Ms. Vancamp, there are state laws that protect you and your baby, and the prison is mandated to provide prenatal care to you while you are detained if you do not want this."

"I want it," I said, cutting her off.

She paused and looked at me. "What about the father?"

"That's the reason," I whispered.

"Come again?" She stared at me over the rim of her glasses.

"Never mind. Look. I'm sure, okay?" I stated this firmly, so she got it.

"Alrighty. Just doing my job. Come with me."

I was then escorted into a room with a bed, a sink, and lots of surgical machinery. The two prison guards waited outside. I gave a blood and urine sample. I was told by the same nurse to undress and put on a hospital gown and lie on the bed. I did so and prayed this would be quick. But it was far from quick.

I was hooked up to an IV that stung and burned.

She then said, "You'll have to have an ultrasound to determine just how far along you are and to make sure it's not an ectopic pregnancy."

I nodded and closed my eyes, not wanting to see anything they saw on their monitor. As they poured the cold gel and used some cold object to prod and press down on my stomach, I attempted to place my mind elsewhere. I counted silently, recited the ABC's forward and backward. I did anything and everything I could think of to keep my mind occupied.

A few minutes later, the doctor finally came into the room. The nurse whispered something to him, and he turned to me.

"You are over sixteen weeks. Because of how far along you are, the baby is larger at this stage of the pregnancy; therefore, the cervix needs to be opened more than for a vacuum curettage. I have to make the uterus contract, and we will then deliver the baby and placenta. So, I pretty much have to induce labor. "

"What? I don't want to have to go through all of that!" I objected.

"Well, it's your choice not to go through with it. But if you want to terminate this pregnancy, this is the only option for you."

"Then what will you do once the baby comes out?"

"Don't concern yourself with that. The fetus won't be alive because of what will be injected into it."

I closed my eyes and nodded. I didn't want to hurt the embryo. I was hoping it would be a simple procedure. But nothing about my fucked-up life was ever simple. And that was all on me. So, after I was induced, I was forced to endure painful contractions, and the nurse in my ear yelling for me to push. The next thing I knew, I was pushing an already dead fetus out of myself.

One of Arianna's son's, Ashlynn, was tugging at my hands, and it brought me back to the present.

"Someone seems to like you, and he never likes anyone," Arianna said, laughing.

I looked down at her adorable twin, who was frowning at me. Then he dashed away, making Arianna laugh some more. I couldn't bring myself to laugh, but I forced a smile.

"What's wrong?" she asked. Arianna was good at reading me.

I looked away. At one point, all of this was on the horizon. I was set to marry a doctor. Everything Arianna had, I was close to having before she did. I shook my head regretfully. The last thing I'd ever expected to do was have to abort my brother's baby. It really did something to me.

Arianna continued to study my face. "I'm sorry, Alexis. I didn't mean to bring it up. But I only say it to tell you that you have to believe with you getting out that God is indeed giving you a second chance."

"And while I may not deserve it, I'm so grateful for one."

"You did your time, so now it's time to move forward with your life. Find love and have some babies. I can have Jabari fix you up with someone. He knows a lot of good, successful men because of his field. In fact, there is this friend. A little rough around the edges, but once you get to know him, he is quite a character. Handsome, funny, successful . . ."

"And you think he would be interested in me?"

"Of course. Why wouldn't he?"

"This ain't the old days where I was working for my dad. Girl, I'm a felon now."

"Oh. I forgot all about that." She nodded then tossed her right hand. "Still, let me work my magic. You were and still are an amazing person. We all have flaws. I told you he was rough around the edges."

"As long as it's no one in law enforcement," I joked. "No. Honestly, right now I'm not ready to date. I wanna get myself together first."

She threw herself in my arms and said ecstatically, "Well, I'm glad that you're home. And my hubby owes me a night out, so keep a Friday open for me."

I laughed and hugged her right back. "I'm so happy I'm home too. And more importantly, I'm glad our friendship was restored. Thank you for forgiving me and being there for me all these years."

"Of course. Besties forever!" she said.

I laughed.

Chapter 5

I'd been thinking about my relationship with Bria. I was determined to set it right. Thing was, no matter how hard it would be, I had to figure out a way to fix it. I couldn't give up. Even if she didn't hear what I wanted to say, I needed to make her listen. I didn't know what I would say or how I would say it, but I needed to begin the process of healing with her.

It was better to start sooner rather than later, so after leaving Arianna's, I drove over to Bria's home. My mother had written her address on a slip of paper with the words *God will lead the way* written at the top. The address put me in estates in Paramount. When I pulled up, I saw her car outside. I knew it had to be hers, because it was a Charger with the license plate *Bria Sexy*. I chuckled to myself. Becoming the first lady of the church or having a baby hadn't changed Bria. I wondered if she ever drove it to the church, and I imagined the shocked look on the faces of the parishioners as she pulled in and they read the license plate.

I knocked on the door softly just in case the baby was asleep. I waited a few moments and listened to hear anyone beyond the door but heard nothing. I knocked softly again. Still no answer.

I walked over to a side window that was open. The wind was blowing the linen curtain back and forth. I peered inside at what looked like the living room. I was about to call my sister's name when I saw her run into the living room. She was buck naked and giggling like a school girl. Startled and embarrassed, I ducked a little to conceal myself from my sister. A man came running into the room, chasing after her. He was completely naked, and his erection was standing at full attention. My eyes widened.

"Come here," he said. "Why you running from me?"

Next thing I knew, he picked her up and placed her on the white rug in the center of the room. In a matter of seconds, he had mounted my sister and started hammering her with his dick. She screamed in ecstasy at the top of her lungs. I gasped and looked away because the last thing I ever wanted to see was Bria having sex. What was most shocking was the man pounding her was not her husband.

I leaned against the house, not sure what to do. My sister having an affair while her baby was in the house. Was she that grimy? I didn't know much about her marriage or her at this point, but I wondered why she was cheating. Did she not love her husband? It was bold of her to be having such an open affair in her own home. Did she not care about her husband finding out? I wasn't judging, because I'd been just as bad and cheated on a great man. What should I do with this information?

Not wanting to hear the passionate screams of my sister and the pounding of flesh, I got in my car and went home. My reconciliation with my sister would have to wait. Maybe my mother had some information about Bria's marriage to help me make sense of what I'd witnessed.

My mother was standing over the stove, stirring something in a pot when I got home.

"Hey, Mom."

"Hey, babe."

"What are you in here doing?"

"I made some pot roast and baked chicken, some fingerling potatoes, and a pot of homemade green beans."

"Is someone coming over?"

"No. It's for us."

I chuckled. "Mom, you don't have to keep making this much food for me."

"Let me pamper my baby. You been locked up for five years. Now go in the dining room and I will bring your food to you."

When I didn't immediately leave the kitchen, she shoved me. I chuckled and obeyed her, making my way to the dining room. I looked at one of the platters on my way out. It had succulent pieces of roast chicken covered in gravy. The setup was like she was entertaining.

"At least let me bring out one of these platters, Mom."

"No. I told you I got this. It will make me feel good, Alexis. Baby, let me."

I smiled and did as she requested.

When I got to the dining room, there was a chocolate cake, a cheesecake, and a sweet potato pie sitting on the table. There was also a platter on the table with seasoned potatoes and green beans with sausage, bacon, and onion. It smelled heavenly. This was the type of food I would daydream about when I was in prison. Crazy part was I worked in the kitchen at the prison, but it was always the same mundane meals I had to cook with not much flavor.

I sat down, shook my head, and smiled. Seconds later, my mother came out with another platter. She placed it on the table and started serving me. I laughed as my mom placed an oversize portion of everything on the table on my plate. I didn't stop her. If it made her feel good to do it, why not?

She then made herself a small plate. Once she sat down and we began eating, she asked, "So, what did you do today?"

I chewed on a piece of roast that was really flavorful and said, "Well, you know, I met with my parole officer first."

"How did the bitch act?"

"The same way she acted when she came over. Bossy, condescending, and disrespectful, Mom."

My mom shook her head. "Why don't we file a complaint against her? I don't see why we have to put up with that shit."

My mom had never been to prison before, so she just didn't understand how things went. Complaints did nothing in the system, and it was probably the same with parole.

I changed the subject. "I also stopped by Arianna's home."

"Did you?" My mom gave a soft smile. "And how was that for you?"

"It was nice, I guess, to meet her husband and her beautiful boys, see how lovely her home is. But then I kept thinking that could have been Dannon and I if I had not—" I shook my head and cleared my throat. I didn't want to cry, and I didn't want my mother to feel sorry for me.

"Anyhow, her family is just gorgeous, and her home is so nice! Huge, but cozy at the same time. It was exactly what I would have expected of her."

My mom looked down but tried to keep the smile on her face. She had been disappointed when Dannon and I didn't work out. She had wanted us to get married and have children. I think the life that Arianna had was the life my mother had always wanted for me. I wondered if I would ever be able to tell my mother about the abortion. Probably not.

"Then I went over to Bria's house."

My mom scoffed at the mention of Bria's name. "I tell you, I just don't know what is going on with that girl. When the baby was born, I stayed with her for a month—Oh, hell. Let me stop. I was supposed to stay for a month, but I barely made it to two weeks. One day, it was like *I* had given birth to that baby, I tell you. I was getting up all hours of the night, feeding the baby, changing the baby, cleaning the house, washing clothes all while her lazy ass slept and fucked that sad husband of hers."

I almost choked on the mouthful of food when she mentioned her husband. I didn't want to mention what I had seen to my mother. I thought it best to keep it to myself for the time being. I figured I'd try to get a clearer picture of what was going on with Bria's marriage before I told my mother anything. The truth was, Bria has always been a wild child of sorts, but I would have thought she'd calm down after getting married and having a child. I wondered why she got married in the first place, since she obviously wasn't ready.

It made me sad to think I might have been able to help her the previous five years and talk with her about troubles she was having in her relationship, but she never wrote, took my calls, or came to see me. I understood her reaction, though. I probably would have done the same thing if I was her. Bria had a monkey on her back because of me. When she slept with Santana, I could have chosen to throw his ass out; instead, I chose to discard Bria from my life. I was stupid, I know. It should have been the other way around.

My mother's voice took me out of my thoughts.

"The day she made it to two weeks post-partum, she put her belly button piercing back in and was out running the streets and leaving me with the baby. And that's not the worst of it, Alexis." Her eyes got wide, and she gripped the fork in her hand like a weapon, jabbing the air as she spoke. "I remember one day, I was cleaning up her room, and I discovered there was another room connected to her room. Don't you know she always had the room locked? Hell, I thought it was a closet at first and maybe it was locked because it had some sort of valuables in it like jewelry or money. But one day, Bria was in a hurry to get her hot ass out the house before I woke up so I couldn't tell her no. And in her haste, she left it unlocked. Well, I went in there and always wished I hadn't, because what I saw still traumatizes me." My mom dramatically placed a hand in the air then to her face before saying, "It was a room with all kinds of satanic sex shit in it."

I looked at my mom, surprised. "Come again?"

"She had at least twenty plastic dicks in different colors, some skinny, some short, some fat, some long, some damn near the size of her little ass. Horse-dick dildos! Whips, chains, handcuffs . . . she even had a muzzle in there! There were ropes hanging from all sides of the room. Three damn stripper poles. And something made like a swing. I even saw some paddles. And all around the walls were nude pictures of my child, busting it wide open, with fingers in her mouth, ass. . . . Well, you get the picture. That goddamn room smelled like a fish market! My heart started beating so fast I ran out the room and fell down the stairs. After that, I couldn't take it. I had to get out of there. I gave her money to get a housekeeper to help her with the house and told her as far as the baby goes, she was on her own! Then I took my ass home. But no matter what, I couldn't stop having nightmares about the shit I saw in that room. It was just too freaky."

I stifled a giggle. So, my sister was a still wild one! Who would have thought she was something like out of that book *Fifty Shades of Grey*? I had read that while locked up. It got me through some very lonely, horny days let's just say. I looked down so my mom didn't see my face as I thought back to those nights reading the book.

"That is not the worst of your sister. You should see the congregation. Matter of fact, I won't even speak on it."

"Speak on what?"

Both my mother's and my head shot up at the intrusion of a visitor who stood in the dining room doorway. I gasped, and my mom screamed.

Chapter 6

"Y'all look like y'all seen a mothafucking ghost."

Santana walked briskly toward the table and sat down across from me, and without hesitation, he grabbed a plate and started serving himself.

He winked at me. "Welcome home, baby."

For a second, I felt weak, my breathing was ragged, and heat rushed to my body at the sight of Santana. But it was not the heat he used to bring out of me. It was the heat of fear, humiliation, and anxiety. Then, as the heat faded, my body went numb.

"Get the fuck out of my house!" my mom blasted.

He pulled the sweet potato pie close to him and stabbed it with his fork. He then placed a huge piece in his mouth, closed his eyes, and acted like he was savoring the pie. He opened his eyes and continued to chew. Now he was smacking his lips. It was a complete sign of disrespect to my mother.

As he chewed, he said, "You need more salt in the crust, and the sweet potatoes needs just a bit more cinnamon. You know, someone told me you supposed to save your nutmegs for pies and cinnamon. What the fuck am I talking about? You threw me away, bitch! I have no family recipes!" His fist slammed down hard on the table.

"Alexis," my mom said evenly, "get up from the table and go in your room while I call the police."

Santana stood, laughed, and sang, "Fuck the police! Fuck the police!" In one swift movement, he knocked all the items off the table. Food, plates, and silverware went flying to the floor.

My mom screamed, got up quickly, and ran from the dining room. "Alexis, go in your room! I'm getting my phone and calling the police."

I stood from the table and backed up. My heart was thudding in my chest.

He winked at me and stood.

I silently shook my head.

As he backed out of the room, he whispered, "Get used to seeing me." Then he gave me a scowl.

I could hear my mom run back into the dining room, yelling, "Yes, I have an intruder in my home. Can you please send someone?"

By the time my mother gave them the address, Santana was out the door.

Santana was nowhere in sight when the police arrived. My mom sat with the police and gave them all of Santana's information. The officers took photos of the broken plates, silverware, and food strewn across the dining room floor. They said they would fill out a report and would be charging Santana with breaking and entering and property damage. I sat there tight-lipped, trying to process what had happened. They advised us to go down to the courts Monday and file a restraining order.

After the police left, my mom paced back and forth in the living room while I sat on the couch.

"I cannot believe he had the nerve to show up here. I can't believe something evil like him came out of me." She slapped one of her hands into the other.

Being a love-sick puppy over that man like he was a drug I was addicted to, then to find out he was my brother had been enough to snap some sense into my ass. Honestly, with everything that had happened, I never expected to see him again. And I never wanted to. I wanted to put the memories of him and everything about that time behind me. I prayed to God that he never bothered me again, although I had a feeling that this mess was far from over and he was far from done bothering me. Truthfully, I wished he was the one I had killed and not that man in the hotel room. With all the problems he had caused my family and me, he deserved to die. Now, he definitely should have been aborted!

I looked around the room at all the mess he had made of such a delicious meal that must have taken my mother all day to cook. I wasn't going to waste anymore of her day, that was for sure. It was on me.

"Mom, go ahead and go to bed. I'll clean up this mess."

"Alexis, I can't sleep. My sleeping ain't been no good in years. How could I ever justify a full night's rest with my baby locked up in that place? I sure wish your father was here to deal with his ass. I might just get a man in my life so he can kick his ass!"

We cleaned up the mess in silence. It was a shame to throw out all the delicious food. When everything was clean and back in its place, I hugged my mother and kissed her cheek.

"I love you, Ma." I said.

"I love you too, baby."

Each of us went to our separate rooms. I tossed and turned all night. Even when I fell asleep, Santana invaded my nightmares. I was going to have to do something about him or else he'd harass me the rest of my life. But I'm sure just as I couldn't sleep, neither could my mom.

I was up and at it first thing Sunday morning. It would be my first time back in the church I grew up in. I was ready to recommit to God. There was a time that I thought I'd never go back to church. I was feeling sorry for myself and felt that I was the only one suffering. I was at my most selfish during this phase of my life. It wasn't until Whosie taught me that I was not the only person suffering and I wasn't the only person who had made fucked-up decisions in life that I realized how selfish I'd been.

It had been a relatively quiet time for me in the prison after Whosie seemed to have left me alone. I didn't know if it was because I stuck up for myself or because Cashmere was my cellie and crazy as hell. All I knew was that as long as she was around, I was left alone. During the time we were cellies, I confided in Cashmere about my fucked-up life. I was hesitant at first, but after a while in prison, you've just got to unload all your bullshit to someone. So, when you find someone who will listen, you take advantage as long as they will listen.

I just knew that when I was done telling her my life, she was going to be totally disgusted with me. But she listened to my sob story and watched me, expressionless, as I told her I had ruined my life. I would go on and on with my woe-is-me story for hours.

One day, in the middle of one of the many pity parties I threw for myself, she said. "You act like you're the only one with problems. And yes, you did some fucked-up stuff, but some have done worse. Listen, at the age of thirteen, I went from being the apple of my father's eye to a stripper and drug dealer, to raped, to a ho with a pimp, and I was hooked on ex. I'm really no moral compass to use to make yourself feel like further shit. And if that's not the worst of my fucked-up life, I murdered my sister. I didn't intend on killing her, but I hated her, so maybe I did." She shrugged her shoulders and held her arms out. "I had a baby by my pimp and passed it off as my husband's baby, although part of me always knew that Dominique was Black's baby." She shook her head regretfully.

"I tried my hardest to convince my husband the baby was his, but he's no dummy. The kid looked nothing like him. My husband hated my guts and my child. I allowed him to mistreat my child because of the guilt I felt. I also loved him and didn't want to lose him. Well, eventually he left me. Instead of looking after my daughter and making sure she was okay, I kept my ass in bed. I was feeling sorry for myself. I was selfish. I thought I was nothing without a man. Talk about having daddy issues.

"The whole time I was boo-hooing over my piece of shit husband, my daughter was hoeing for my old pimp right under my nose. Then my husband died. I grieved for too long, and now that I look back, I wasn't grieving for him. I was grieving for myself. I felt sorry for myself for being the only one who was suffering in the world. I felt that no one else suffered as much as me. And while I was sitting there grieving, my daughter was getting pimped out." She slapped one hand into the other palm.

"When I snapped out of it, I went in search of my daughter. I found her, and I found him. I lit that dirty mothafucka up. If it wasn't for my baby, I wouldn't care if I had to spend the rest of my life in here. But I have to get out because they locked her up. But one way or another, I got to get out this bitch."

As I reeled from what she said, I sat down next to her and hugged her. The life she lived was horrible. I had never had it that bad, and there I was, dwelling on my situation when she had a child to look after and she couldn't, due to being locked up. From that point forward, I stopped complaining about my life. I took responsibility for my decisions and actions.

I refocused my attention on getting ready for church. I wanted to make a great first impression. I was nervous as hell about going back to my home church. Church is supposed to be a place of forgiveness, but it sure isn't a place without judgement. The good church folk like to say they don't judge, but I knew the deal. It may not have been the best choice for my comfort to go back to that church, but I couldn't see myself setting foot in any other church. I was baptized there, and I did have special memories of attending as a little girl. There was still a love deep down I held for the church.

I remember, as a little girl, memorizing a poem about Jesus and performing it with the other kids in children's church every Easter. All the children would stand in front of the entire congregation and perform. Standing up there preparing to begin, I would search out my parents. When I saw them in the pew, so proud, I smiled so big it would hurt my cheeks. As I got older, singing in the choir with Arianna was some of the happiest times for me. The nerves I felt before my very first solo, "Jesus Loves Me," is something I will never forget. When I finished, I saw my parents weeping with joy and pride.

Of course, once Santana came into the picture, things started to change for me at the church. It was one humiliating event after the next: him shoving Dannon's mother after she lost her only son, and that time when the Jamaicans came in beating Santana's ass. The most humiliating and mean thing was how Justin's secret that he was gay was revealed at my parents' anniversary. Several church members were in attendance, and the word spread fast through the congregation.

I had acted a plum fool, chasing after that man who brought me nothing but destruction. I brought problems to my home church that it just didn't need. I couldn't blame them if they refused my entrance or simply ignored me. I would accept whatever came my way, because I was the cause of it. Five years of prison had definitely taught me how to own my shit.

I sat with my mother in the parking lot, watching the other early parishioners arrive. I debated whether it was best for me to get in there and sit down before too many people showed up, or to wait until the service had started and try to sneak in the back without anyone seeing me.

"We have to go in at some point," my mother said.

"I know. I'm nervous."

"Let go and let God." She patted my knee.

I nodded, took a deep breath, and made my way to the entrance. No one stopped us from entering. However, when we entered, it felt like everyone was staring at us. People shook their heads at us, and there was a whole lot of whispering. I knew why. It was humiliating. My mother had managed to earn back the trust of the parish-

ioners, and my sister had extreme opposition to becoming first lady because of me, and now there I was, back
from prison, the woman who caused so much chaos for
the church. I was almost certain they all knew I had been
sleeping with my brother and killed a man. It was probably the biggest scandal the church had ever heard.

The choir sang "Our God Is Awesome." As I listened,
it reminded me when I was an active member of the
church and singing my heart out. I was always the lead
because I sang so well. I silently sang the words in my
head. I desperately wanted to sing out loud, but the less
attention I brought on myself, the better. Hopefully,
over time things would relax and I could begin to enjoy
singing with the congregation again. I prayed to God for
that to manifest.

*Our God is awesome. He heals me when I'm broken.
Gives strength where I've been weakened. Forever He
will reign.*

While I was locked up, I often sang for the inmates.
They got a kick out of it. They said I sounded like
Jennifer Hudson. I must admit I did miss singing in front
of my church. Standing up there with the choir, I always
knew I looked good in my beautiful church clothes.
Although somewhat conservative, I always made sure
they accentuated my curves. I would spend Saturday
evening making sure my hair, makeup, and nails were
always flawless. Even my heels were killer. And I commanded all attention when I belted out Gospel songs. I
couldn't help but acknowledge the fact that I was cocky
and arrogant back then. Humble, I was not. God blessed
me with a gift—a voice I had should have been grateful
for, not arrogant about. But because it commanded so

much attention, I treated people like it was a gift just to be around me. I was snotty and stuck-up, pretty much a bitch. What an ugly, ugly person I was.

I silently asked God for forgiveness.

After the choir finished singing their selections, my sister and her husband came out. While her husband smiled and waved, my sister said cheerfully, "Welcome back, and to all our visitors, we want to wish you a hearty welcome and a loud praise."

To that, the entire church clapped.

I must admit my sister really made a beautiful first lady. She looked very pretty and chose something really nice to wear. It was a royal blue dress that stopped at her knees with matching blue pointy heels. Her neck and ears sparkled with diamonds. The only thing that made her lose points was the fact there was a long slit in the back, exposing her entire back.

"What is that girl wearing, Father God?" my mother mumbled.

Once everyone was seated, her husband asked, "Do we have any visitors?"

Despite the look I gave my mother, she shook her head at me and stubbornly stood and said, "Well, sort of. My daughter Alexis is home. As you all know, she has been away for over five years. Praise God she is home!"

There were gasps, whispers, and boos. Someone even yelled out, "Anti-Christ!"

I cringed and put my head down.

That was followed up by, "Jezebel, light-skin devil, murderer, incest queen!" And, ironically, *"Black widow."* All while my sister smirked and her husband looked down at his shoes. They were lost, and I was lost as far as what to do. I wasn't exactly ready to be reintroduced at that moment, and I hadn't prepared for it. I was hoping to come to a couple services first and some of the Bible studies and slowly reintegrate myself. But hell, my mom chose to do it her way.

She didn't appear to like all the names I was being called. "Hey! Hey! Hey! Now, listen. You're supposed to be church folk. This is supposed to be a family, and family is supposed to support each other." She looked around the church angrily as it quieted down. "Since when is it okay to judge? Harass? And I'm going to say it like this: I've been a member of this church for a very long time, and my daughters were raised in this church. Both were baptized here, and my entire family did a lot of great things for this church!

"John 8:7 says, 'So when they continued asking him, he lifted up himself, and said unto them, He that is without sin among you, let him first cast a stone at her.' In Matthew:7, 'Do not judge, or you too will be judged. For in the same way you judge others, you will be judged, and with the measure you use, it will be measured to you." She wagged a finger at them. "Just remember, the blind cannot lead the blind. They will both fall into a pit! None of you all are perfect.

"Sister Esther, I heard you call my child a murderer. How much murdering you think that gang-banging son of yours that you continue to uphold has murdered?"

Sister Esther gasped and put her head down in shame.

"That's right! I'm calling you holy rollers out! Since the *pastor* and *first lady* won't. Brother Thomas! You are an alcoholic, and your daughter is a chronic crack cocaine user who sells her ass. Let's whisper about that! First Corinthians, says 'No temptation has overtaken you except what is common to mankind. And God is faithful; he will not let you be tempted beyond what you can bear. But when you are tempted, he will also provide a way out so that you can endure it.'"

To this, Brother Thomas stood and stormed out of the church.

"Bye. Yeah, I know my stuff. Go *find your way out*, Brother Thomas," my mom said.

"Do I have to keep going? So, to all you fools—and I'm telling you right now, what I won't do is stand for any of you hypocritical mothafuckas disrespecting my daughter. Yes, I said it! Mothafuckas. If you're going to go against the Bible and judge, then I will go against the Bible and swear, got damnit! Now, she did her time, and guess what? Y'all are not going to make her do anymore with your condemnation! I refuse to deal with your self-righteousness, that's for sure. Keep at it, and I will for sure get to calling more of you out. Now, she will be attending this church, Bible study, events, and guess what? You will leave her the hell alone!"

Silence was all she was met with. I didn't know if that was because they agreed with my mother or if they didn't want any of their own dirty laundry to be revealed by her. To that my mother sat down.

"Welcome back to church, sister Alexis," Bria's husband said.

"Thank you. I am glad to be back," I said.

"Now, does anyone want to greet Alexis with a hug?"

No one moved. Someone shouted, "Hell to the no!"

I placed my hand over one of my mother's arms so she didn't get up again.

"It's okay, Mom."

Casey said, "There is no need for that, church members. Like sister Debra said, we are a church of love and acceptance. The Bible says, 'In Him we have redemption through His blood, the forgiveness of sins, in accordance with the riches of God's grace.' So, sister Alexis, you have redemption here, and you are always welcome in this church house."

The church was uneasy. A few members got up and left. Others were talking amongst themselves. Casey waited for the parishioners to leave, then resumed the service. As he spoke, the remaining parishioners settled down.

Surprisingly, Casey was really a good pastor. He didn't ramble on. What he said made sense, and it definitely helped me— especially the part, "You're on the verge of a breakthrough. Now, there will be hurdles, but the Bible says steadfast. Don't go to the left; don't go to the right. Stand firm in your purpose." I needed to hear that, because my plan to make things right with everyone was going to be a trying task. I hoped and prayed I'd get the forgiveness I needed.

"Now I am going to hand things over to my wife."

"Thanks, honey. Now, one thing my husband forgot to mention is that as good Christians, it's all about finding ways to humble ourselves." As she spoke, ushers scrambled to add chairs on the pulpit. "In John, we know that Jesus humbled himself and washed the apostles' feet and commanded them to love each other. So, we thought, what would be more fitting than to do as Jesus our Lord and Savior did?"

She unfolded a piece of paper and said, "Can we please have sisters Mary, Clare, and Pamela up here?"

I watched the three women stand. My heart sank when I saw sister Clare stand and make her way to the pulpit. Clare was Dannon's mother, another person I needed to ask forgiveness from. I took a deep breath as the three women took the three chairs on the pulpit.

"Now, can we get three volunteers to wash these women's feet? Come on. Don't be shy, y'all."

No one moved.

"Come on now. Do I have to start calling people? What are you, above Jesus?"

With trembling lips, shaking hands, and a heavy, thudding heart, I stood to my feet, ignoring the gasps around me as I walked to the stage. There were a lot of whispers, but then when my mother said, "All right, don't start it again!" they stopped.

I walked directly in front of Sister Clare. Her eyes were wide at the sight of me. She looked as though she had seen a ghost the same way I had probably looked the day before when I saw Santana.

It was crazy. At one point, Sister Clare had loved me. It was like having a second mom, and she called me her daughter even before Dannon proposed to me. I had a key to her house and could pop in and out whenever I wanted to. And she honestly was always a sweet, sweet woman in general.

Dannon was the light of her life. Many times, she had told me what a miracle baby he was because she had so many miscarriages before him, and right when she was about to give up, she popped up pregnant with Dannon. However, her doctor told her she was not going to be able to carry him to full term. Dannon ended up being born early, due to an emergency C-section, and at one point, he had stopped breathing. As a preemie, he had so many issues that it was not likely he was going to make it. But she said she and her husband prayed over him, and miraculously, he pulled through. It solidified Clare's faith in God.

So, there she was, face to face with me, the woman responsible for her miracle son's death. I wished I had cared more when it first happened. I wished instead of cheating on him, I would have just broken up with him first. I was trying to have my cake and eat it too.

I turned my attention to Ms. Clare. As I kneeled before her, I smiled. "Hi, Clare. I know it's been a while, but I wanted to be the one to wash your feet. It would be an honor for me to do it."

She didn't say anything. She let me take off her pumps and slip her feet into the water. When I say the church was quiet, the church was *quiet!* But even if it wasn't, it wouldn't have mattered to me, because this was something I needed to do. This woman had been done so wrong and she had lost her only child.

I grabbed the washcloth, dipped it in the soapy water, and began gently washing her feet.

"Clare, I just wanted to say thank you so much for allowing me to do this."

She looked like she was struggling with how she should react or even process what was going on. I'm sure she felt a mixture of emotions: anger, hurt, hostility. Maybe even hate. But still, she allowed me to continue what I was doing.

Under ordinary circumstances maybe I should have been embarrassed, but I wasn't. At this point, the way I treated her and allowed Santana to treat her, it was the least I could do. It was a humbling experience to kneel before God, Clare, and the other parishioners and wash her feet. The old me would have felt embarrassed because It would have been beneath me.

"Ma'am, for the past five years being locked up, I prayed for the day to be face to face with you. There has always been one thing I always wanted to tell you, and I am so, so grateful that God has given me this opportunity to do it today."

Her bottom lip trembled a bit.

I continued to wash her feet. "I wanted to say that I am so sorry for the way I treated your son and you. I do realize that does nothing for the pain you will always feel because of your loss."

Tears slid down her face. She stomped one of her feet in the water, splashing it in my face. "H–how could you do that to him? You were everything to my son!"

The church gasped.

I wiped the water away quickly.

"You bitch! There is not a day that goes by that I don't miss my baby!" She shifted her foot forward forcibly, and before I could scoot away, her foot connected with my face. It landed with such force that it knocked me backward and caused me to hit my head on one of the steps.

I attempted to get up, but before I knew it, I felt myself black out.

Chapter 7

Clare Spencer had knocked me unconscious. When I regained consciousness, Casey and my mother were standing over me. They helped me up and escorted me to a back room behind the pulpit. They laid me on an aquamarine velvet couch. Sunlight was shining through the windows behind the couch.

"Can you close the curtains? That sun is so bright," I said.

The room was dark and quiet with the curtains closed.

"How are you? Can I get you anything?" my mother asked.

"My head hurts something awful, and everything is blurry."

Casey brought me a glass of water. "I've got to get back to the church and regain some order on this mess."

I agreed.

"I think we need to get you to the hospital. You took a nasty hit to the head," my mother said.

"I'm fine."

"Oh, yeah? Where are you right now?"

"In prison. Dumb question," I answered.

"All right. We're going to the hospital."

Hours later, I was sitting in a hospital bed, still feeling fuzzy as hell. The room lights were off and the curtains drawn. My mom was seated across from me. When she saw I was up, she took a deep breath.

"You okay?"

I nodded although my head was still aching.

"The doctor said you have a concussion."

I swallowed. "Mrs. Spencer has a mean kick."

My mom chuckled. "Shut up, Alexis."

"I expected a whole lot worse, so I'm okay with her reaction. I wanted to look her in her eyes and tell her how sorry I am for Dannon's death and to take responsibility for how horribly I handled the whole situation."

"Well, I certainly don't know if she is going to forgive you, but that's good that you tried to make amends, baby. I damn near jumped on her when she kicked you, but she claims she didn't do it on purpose."

I took a deep breath, relieved my mom didn't jump on Sister Clare. And to be honest, I didn't care if she had kicked me on accident or on purpose. I deserved a kick. A kick to my head was nowhere near what had happened to Dannon or the pain of her burying her only son.

The doctor came back into the room to check on me. He looked in my eyes, asked me a few questions, gave me some instructions about dealing with a concussion, and discharged me.

I went home with my mom. She tried to lay out a big spread of food for me, but my appetite was gone. I was still feeling pretty terrible. I picked at some of the chicken she had put out, but after a few bites I was done. The doctor had cautioned about nausea due to the concussion, and my stomach was definitely doing flips. There was a chance I could throw up in my sleep and choke myself, something I wanted to avoid. I took a Tylenol to help my headache and went to bed.

The next morning, my mother and I got up extra early and went to the courthouse to file our restraining orders against Santana. My eyes were still sensitive to any light, so I had to wear the biggest, darkest sunglasses I had, even inside. I got some strange looks from people at the courthouse.

The lady helping us fill out the necessary paperwork kept looking at me. I think she thought I was hiding a black eye. Every so often, she would look at me sympathetically and tell me she was sorry I was going through this ordeal. When we got to the end of the form it became clear that we were going to have a problem. The last known address we had for Santana was useless. He had moved from there, and we had no clue where he was, which meant that he couldn't be formally served. We were able to get the restraining order filed, but it wouldn't become official until he was properly served. It was so frustrating, and my mother was so pissed off.

From there, I left to have lunch with a dear friend, Justin. Over and over, I thanked God that my relationship with him and Arianna was preserved. We had both hoped that Arianna could meet us, but her twins were nursing a cold. Of all relationships, I never thought this one would have been repairable. After Santana revealed Justin's secret, forcing him to come out of the closet, I thought for sure Justin would disown me. The only reason I told Santana was so he wouldn't be jealous of the time I spent with Justin. It took Justin a while to get over it, and truthfully, Arianna had a lot to do with it, but eventually he forgave me. I was so grateful to both of them for being such strong friends.

Justin and I met over at The Kickin' Crab in Buena Park. Man, it felt so good to hug him. And when he pulled away from me and looked at me, all that hurt from the night Santana had humiliated him was washed away. All I saw was love.

He lifted me in his arms and spun me around.

I squealed. "Justin, put me down!"

He did and laughed. "It's just so good to see you. Come on, girl."

Since we were going during the day, there really was no wait for us.

"Prison made you way too skinny. I'm going to fatten you up."

I laughed again. "You and my mom."

We feasted on king crab legs, fried shrimp, garlic noodles, and Cajun fries. I stared at the food in all its glory. I hadn't had seafood in years! I had adjusted to chicken and pork products while locked up and never thought I'd see a piece of seafood ever again. It had been so long, I didn't even know how to crack the crab. I watched Justin then followed his lead, starting with a claw.

"I've damn near forgot how to eat crab," I said.

"Well, that's okay, baby girl. It just makes you more fierce. Sorry I couldn't make it for your homecoming," he said after placing a piece of crab in his mouth.

I placed a succulent piece in my mouth and closed my eyes, savoring the taste of the zesty kickin'-style sauce and the tender, buttery taste of the crab. *Heaven.*

"That's okay, Justin. I'm just so glad to see you outside of prison."

He threw both his hands in the air. "Yes, Lord!"

To that, we both busted up laughing. Then his face turned serious.

"To tell the truth, although the coming out was a little unorthodox, I am so glad that the world now knows. The church semi accepted me back, and so did my family. But I feel so free now that it is out. Even when I was lashing out at you, I was glad it was out. The burden of shame is gone, and I can live a free gay man!"

That felt so good to hear. I clapped for him. "That's really great, Justin. I'm so happy that they did sort of. But I'm sure in no time, they will come around."

"That would be good. But what's even better is that I don't care if they ever do. I've accepted myself, and that's what matters. Self-love is always the best. I wave my gay flag proudly."

"How'd you do it?" I asked. "How'd you get to this point?"

"I let go and don't care what others think of me. The only people that matter are my friends and family, and frankly, if any of them can't accept me, then they can kick rocks right out my life. There are plenty of people in this world who think I'm fabulous and will accept me for me."

I was so proud of my friend for getting to this point. I wondered if I'd ever feel peace and resolution in my life again. I wondered if I'd ever get to the point that I didn't care what others thought of me and my transgressions.

"So, what is the plan, Miss Alexis? Now that you got your life back, what do you plan on doing?"

Before I could respond, he said energetically, "Singing?"

I laughed. "Justin, no! Unless you're talking about church, and I think I would be pushing it. They barely wanted to let me in there this past Sunday."

"Baby girl, if they let me back in the door, you will be fine. You didn't kill that man on purpose. This ain't the first scandal the church has witnessed. And, chile, they need help in the choir—amongst other things."

"What other things?" I asked.

"Chile, in time you will see. Now, back to singing in church."

"Hmmm. If it helps my sister out, then I won't object."

I started to tell him the stress I was having with the fact that Santana came to my mother's house, plus my shady parole officer, but I didn't want to darken the day. It felt so good to be able to catch up with my friend and not worry about time constraints like I did when I was locked up.

Chapter 8

The next Sunday, I was resolved to get back to church. I really needed the church in my life at that time, and I wasn't going to let one crazy Sunday stop me from attending. I was hoping that after a week everyone had a chance to calm down and forgive me for my sins.

I checked myself in the mirror one last time and left the house. My mother had already left because she was volunteering in the children's church that week. She was scheduled to be on for all the masses starting at eight thirty that morning. I only planned on attending the ten thirty service.

I called Justin earlier that morning to get him to come, but he bailed because he was nursing a hangover. Since I didn't know how they would receive me, I was hoping he would be able to come for extra support. That boy was living his best life, for sure.

As I stopped at a red light, my cell beeped, indicating I had a text message.

I looked down at the phone and read the text from a number I didn't recognize.

Dumb bitch. Pull over in the parking structure and then take your dumb ass in the Denny's and sit down fore I follow you to church.

My heartbeat sped up and my hands became shaky on the steering wheel. I looked around at the cars surrounding me at the light, looking for Santana. I didn't recognize anyone. Where was he? I contemplated ignoring the text and heading to church, but considering the drama I caused last week and the ruckus I knew Santana was capable of, I followed the instructions. I could not have him enter the church and cause more problems. I really wanted to become a member of the church again.

I pulled in the shopping center. It was busy with Sunday church folk going for breakfast. It took a moment for the hostess to seat me. As I waited for a table to clear, I kept scanning the restaurant for Santana.

"Excuse me," someone said behind me.

I jumped.

"I'm sorry. I didn't mean to startle you," the handsome father said. He was holding his daughter's hand.

"It's fine," I said.

"Are you waiting to be seated?" he asked.

"Yes."

"Oh, thanks. Busy this morning, huh?"

"Yes." I tried to cut the conversation short, although I couldn't help looking at his ring finger and noticing it was missing a ring.

The hostess came back with a menu. "Right this way," she said. "I'll be right with you, sir." She gave him a flirtatious smile.

He smiled. "Enjoy your meal," he said as I walked away.

"You too."

The hostess sat me at a booth. Seconds later, Santana came striding into the restaurant. "What's up, baby?" He stared down at me as he lowered himself into the booth, sitting across from me.

I said nothing. To think that once I used to love this man . . . was completely obsessed with him. I thought he was all of all, worth losing everyone and everything in my life. Worth shutting people out and putting those I loved down. And even after losing everything, including my freedom, I had still wanted this man. At that time, I didn't know who he really was, as far as being my brother, or the fact that our relationship was never real to him but just a plot. I thought of how he had caused so many problems with the people in my life. I mean, not one single person in my life was unaffected by him. That should have been an indication for me that he was bad news. Also, he did not treat me right. I mean, he slept with my sister! Had women over the house. And still there I was, his little sprung fool, losing my dad's trust, my job, home, my best friend. And still, I was back for more—willing, able, and accepting of more bad treatment when I knew better. It was like he was my drug and I was highly addicted to him.

But not anymore. I now despised this man. I know it's wrong to say, but I hated him. I mean, he was evil at its finest. He knowingly slept with his sister and tried to ruin my life, and he taunted me after he did this. As much as I was against abortion, I knew for a fact I had made the right choice not bringing a child by him into the world, that's for sure. I would just continue to pray that God would forgive me.

His harsh tone took me out of my thoughts. "Oh, you not going to speak? I mean, damn, I'm trying to be nice to your ass."

Was he out of his damn mind? He had set me up and tried to destroy me and my entire family. Had just mobbed into my mother's house and made a complete mess of dinner by shoving it on the floor! And here he was yet again. What was his angle? What did he want from me? I closed my eyes briefly and held in a breath before letting it out slowly to stop myself from crying. This man had so much nerve. Too much!

"H–hi, Santana," I was able to get out.

"Now, that's better. You know, at one point you didn't have a problem speaking and saying my name." He winked. "You used to yell it like you were on a rooftop. Don't you remember that? All the times I made you feel good? Made you nut?"

I looked away, disgusted. I didn't want to think about the times I had sex with Santana. It made my stomach churn.

"Well, Alexis, it's good you beat that murder case and you're out and free. Now, the way that shit went down . . . don't take it personal. You were just a casualty of war. It could have ended a lot worse, baby girl. You could have gotten the death penalty, spent the rest of your life behind bars, but you didn't. Let that shit go and count your blessings."

My eyes widened. I couldn't believe he had no type of remorse for the things he had done!

"Now, let's get to the point. Plain and simple, you and your silly-ass sister had what I always wanted. Man, what I craved. A mother. A nice upbringing. Maybe I didn't go about getting it the right way, but at the time, my mind was on some fuck-the-world type of shit. That's what motivated me day by day. To get back at, to hurt who I felt had hurt me. And you may feel that that wasn't you, but it was. You were given a charmed life that I deserved too. I was our mama's first born. I should have had the opportunities you had, the love you had all these years. I was angry and bitter. Out for blood. And then there was another side of me that yearned for my mother's love. I wanted it more than anything. But hell, back then I put revenge over the desire to have my biological mother in my life.

"Now, looking back, I wish that I had done things differently. Came at you guys differently. Not slept with you or your little sister. Crazy part is there is a part of me that hates her and a part of me that loves her . . . and a part of me that really wants her to love me." He looked away when he said the last part.

"Alexis, plain and simple, I want to know my mom. Your mom. Our mom. And I need you to make it happen for me. I need you to reintroduce me to the fam and . . . Well, I want to be a part of it. I want to be an older brother to you and Bria and a loving devoted son to Mom."

Was this man insane? No, he was past insane. He had knowingly slept with his two sisters, got my little sister on drugs, set me up, and now he was sitting in front of me asking to be a part of our family or what was left of it. I don't think I have ever met anyone as deranged as Santana Marcelino. And the truth was my mother did not want anything to do with him—son or not, flesh and blood or not. She hated him. She had told me that on several occasions for the past five years. There was nothing I could do to change that, and I wouldn't sit here and pretend that I could. I didn't care if it hurt him.

"So, what do you say?" He looked at me eagerly, like a small child asking his parents to buy them a toy or a damn ice cream cone.

"What is it that you want?"

His eyes got crazy. "You didn't hear what the fuck I just said?"

"I heard you, but I don't believe it. What is it that you really want?"

"Alexis, I'm serious. I want to be a family. I want Mom to put me through college and let me run the businesses. I want us to get together all the time. Be inseparable. I want to be loved. I mean, we can go slow if you think that will be better. We can take baby steps. I want you to start inviting me over for dinner. Start out small, like weekly Sunday dinner. We can call it Soul Food Sundays. I know once she takes the time to get to know me, she will see me different. I know for a fact I can win her over once Mom gets a chance to see me for who I truly am. I'm not a bad person. I mean, you of all people should know. I made you fall in love with me, remember? In fact, I can bring some of those sculptures you fell in love with when we first met. Remember?"

I didn't respond, so he kept going.

"I'm that same personality that won you and your sister over. I'm charming, handsome, funny, charismatic. That has got to have an impression on her as well. We just need to put the past behind us."

This man was out of his damn mind. None of us wanted any parts of him. I couldn't believe he would think anyone would after all that he had caused.

He eyed me, looking extremely hopeful. If I wasn't scared he would do something to hurt me, I would have laughed in his face.

"Ummmm. I don't think—"

"Hold the fuck up! I just poured out my heart to you, and you starting this sentence with 'I don't think'? Well, let me tell you what I think. I think you should be really careful about your next set of words. Matter of fact, answer my question only. Are you gonna do it?"

There just wasn't an opportunity for anything he wanted to ever come to fruition. Maybe if he had come into our lives differently, been right, and not come for revenge, not come for blood—then maybe what he was seeking, he might have gotten, despite the clause my mother had in her adoption. But he didn't come that way. He came with a vendetta, seeking to hurt and ruin our lives. He had almost destroyed my family. There was no way she would allow this.

Therefore, without hesitation, I looked him in his eyes and said calmly, "No."

And without hesitation, spit flew from his mouth and directly into my face.

I gasped, closed my eyes, and struggled to pull a napkin out the dispenser on the table to wipe his saliva off my face. I scraped my face with the napkin and then looked his way fearfully, hiding my disgust for fear he would do something worse to me.

At this point, he was walking toward the exit.

I looked around to see if anyone had seen what happened. I was pretty sure I looked humiliated. And yes, people saw. A few of the customers had even paused their eating and were looking our way. But no one said anything.

I stood and made my way to the restroom. Once there, I splashed cold water and hand soap on my face, rinsed it off with more water, and dried my face off with a paper towel. Through the entire process, my hands couldn't stop shaking, and I couldn't stop crying. I felt embarrassed and scared. I didn't want Santana anywhere near my family anymore, and I knew for a fact that my mother would feel the same. The situation was too far gone to fix, but I doubted he would see it that way. He was a dangerous man, and I was scared as hell of him. And he was so, so dirty. There was no way he could ever justify sleeping with both of his sisters and trying to destroy both of us to get to my mother. Ugh! He wanted to hurt my family due to being given up for adoption.

My shoulders shuddered. I had no idea of the best way to deal with the situation. I didn't know who could help me. As frightened as I was of the man, I was determined not to let him hurt my family or me anymore.

Chapter 9

I tried to block out what had happened at Denny's as I headed to the doors of the church. As I did, visions of the incident were before my eyes, and I felt myself tearing up again. I wiped the tears away quickly, sniffed, and reached for the door handle. Before I could open the door, it was pulled open, and I came face to face with Dannon's mother. Caught off guard, I smiled nervously, not knowing what she would do to me.

"Hi Mrs.—"

Before I could finish, she grabbed both of my hands in hers, and her eyes shined in the corners with tears. "I forgive you, Alexis. I forgive you."

My heart sped up at her choice of words as a feeling of relief and gratitude flooded throughout my body. It was not something I was expecting. To know that she forgave me for what I had done completely wiped away what had happened earlier.

I said, "Thank you." I leaned over and embraced her. And how crazy, she hugged me back—a super snug, tight hug.

I entered the church and took a seat in the back row. Before the service began, I got down on my knees and prayed to God for his mercy. I couldn't believe Dannon's mother had forgiven me. It could only have been by God's intervention.

Later that evening, I gave my hair one last smooth-over and looked myself over in the mirror.

"You look cute."

I smiled and looked at my mother standing behind me in the mirror.

"Thanks, Mom." This was really the first time that I was going out since I'd been released from prison and really the first time I had gotten dressed up and put on makeup since my release. I was invited out by Jabari to Arianna's birthday party at The Reef in Long Beach. I wore a striped black-and-white dress and a pair of black pumps. My hair was flat-ironed and hung down my back. I also applied blush, lipstick, and mascara.

I was excited to be going out but also nervous. How had everything changed since I'd been away? What was the latest drink, the latest trends? Who else would be there, and what did they know about me?

My thoughts were interrupted by my mother's voice. "You look apprehensive. You need to go and have a good time. You look beautiful. But if you're uncomfortable with the scar on your neck, I'm sure I can find a cute turtleneck."

"No, Mom, it's fine." People had been looking at the scar or my neck for the longest, so I was used to it. And it was going to forever be a part of me. I wasn't ashamed of it.

"When did you become so brave?"

I laughed as I thought back to prison.

One day, Cashmere had snapped. I mean really snapped. We were both in the chow line getting our meal. All I know is a lady who had just arrived with blond hair and a tat on her neck that said Mccay bumped into Cashmere and said, "You'll pay for what you did to Black, bitch."

That's when Cashmere spun around with her tray. "Fuck Black!" She slammed it into the woman's face. Then Cashmere rushed her, knocking the lady off her feet.

From the corner of my eye, I saw another woman with the same tattoo on her neck rush toward Cashmere, holding a shank. As my heart sped up, I forced myself not to run. I thought quick, and instead, I snuck up behind her and curled an arm around the girl's neck. I then used my other hand to grip the shank she had. I applied as much pressure as I could to her neck.

In a shaky voice, I said, "Don't even think about it, bitch."

She headbutted me backward, busting my lip. I stumbled but ignored the pain. She used the diversion to wiggle out of my hand. She rushed toward me with gritted teeth and started swinging. Although my heart was still pounding, I placed my two balled fists in the air. Even though I had fought Whosie, the fear remained. Still, I swung, missed, and got drilled. I threw a kick that landed in her midsection and caused her to stumble.

From the corner of my eye, I saw Cashmere continue to punch the woman in her face so hard and so fast the girl was bleeding and couldn't get in one hit in retaliation. I rushed up to the girl as she was crouched over and started punching her in her head so hard I could feel my nails breaking. But I kept going, and we were going blow for blow at this point, but I didn't stop swinging. The prison guards warned us to stop. Cashmere continued to swing, and so did I, until the guards started spraying us. Then it was over.

We all had to stay in the SHU as punishment, but I was so proud of myself that I stood up for her and didn't allow her to be jumped. From that point forward, it had become nothing to me to fight.

I smiled at my mother. "I was placed in a lot of situations where I was forced to respond, Mom. If I were to back down from a fight now, it would strictly be so I didn't get arrested, not based on fear."

"You were in a very tough place. I didn't think any of my babies could make it in there. I thought you were going to break. I'm proud you didn't. So then, you still don't seem like you want to go. Why?"

What my mom didn't understand was that I couldn't help but see the person in the prison garb. I still saw a convict. That was the crazy part. It would take me a while to get back to feeling like the old Alexis. I mean, that was if I could. I had seen a lot of craziness and participated in a lot of craziness. The old Alexis was dead—as she should have been.

"If you're having doubts, worries, stress, or all of them, I wish you wouldn't. You earned this—the right to look pretty and enjoy yourself. You did your time, baby, and now the time is here for you to enjoy the rest of your life while you still got one, not dwell on anyone or anything." She paused. "And if you're worried about that bastard, don't. I have the security cameras hooked back up, and if he comes our way, I will have something for his ass."

Yes, that, too, was a concern. What my mother didn't realize was that he didn't need to come to the house to bother me. And she didn't know that he already had. And man, I didn't want to tell her something that would stress her out.

I cracked a smile and told her, "You're right, Mom. I'm going to go and enjoy myself." I grabbed my purse and keys and walked out of my bedroom.

"Have fun!"

"Thanks!"

Once I got to the restaurant, I struggled to find some-where to park. After nearly fifteen minutes, I was begin-ning to panic because Jabari wanted everyone there before them so the surprise wouldn't be ruined. Just as I was thinking I'd have to wait it out until later so I didn't ruin anything, I saw a car backing out.

Yes, I said to myself. *I have a spot!* I grabbed my purse and quickly got out of the car. As I opened the door, the handle slipped out of my hands and my door slammed into the car next to me.

"What the—!"

I got out of the car and looked up at a man, sneering and yelling at me.

"You just going to stand there? Dumb ass! You just hit my goddamn car!"

"I'm sorry. I—"

"You're sorry? Sorry doesn't take the scratch off my mothafucking car! Just watch what the fuck you're doing, stupid. It's just that simple."

I had spent five years in prison, and during that time, I was called out of my name more than my own damn name. Some stuff was serious, and some was trivial. Prison had taught me to choose my battles wisely. As much as this asshole was pissing me off, I knew I couldn't fight him. So, I stormed away, ignoring his childish ass!

When I made it to the entrance of the restaurant, I took a deep breath before stepping inside. I wasn't going to let that incident taint my night. I put a smile on my face and opened the door to the restaurant. Everything looked so beautiful. It was decorated in the colors of pink and silver. There were balloon bouquets and flowers all over the room. There were pictures of Arianna pretty much everywhere and a huge banner that said: HAPPY BIRTHDAY ARIANNA.

Jabari had hired a DJ and a band. There was a dessert bar with items like cupcakes, cake pops, and deep friend cheesecake, pastries, and cookies—all of Arianna's favorites.

As nervous as I was to be there, I was happy I was home to be able to experience this. I had missed so many birthdays, and she didn't get a chance to experience any of my birthdays while I was locked up.

Arianna's husband wanted me to sing, so I decided to speak to the band about my thoughts. They were all cool and were down to try out my ideas. We decided to go off to a quiet spot so I could give them an idea of what I was thinking. When I finished singing for them, they all went crazy for my voice. It soothed a lot of the fears I had about singing and the judgment I was anticipating from some of the guests.

I didn't recognize any of the other people at the party. It must have been people that Arianna had made friends with after I went away, or many of Jabari's crew. Feeling a little uncomfortable about not knowing anyone, I sat down at an empty table. As I admired the sparkly centerpiece, a photographer popped up in my face and said quickly before flashing, "Smile."

I did, but I knew it probably looked tight.

As the photographer walked away from me, Arianna's mother stood in the center of the room and said, "Okay. They are coming, so get ready to yell surprise!"

I made my way to the band. I stood in front of them, taking deep breaths to calm my nerves. The doors were opened, and Jabari walked in with Arianna, who was blindfolded. Once the blindfold was pulled off, everyone yelled "Surprise!" Arianna looked around and screamed. The band started playing, and I stepped up to the mic.

The song Jabari wanted me to sing was Prince's "Most Beautiful Girl in The World." As I sang, Arianna blew me kisses, and then her husband pulled her onto the dance floor. I belted out the song like I'd never stopped singing and was able to hit all the right notes.

Family and friends crowded around Arianna and clapped and whistled for them as they danced. Arianna looked beautiful in a white silk dress that gave her this floating effect as she moved. Her hair hung in very neat, tight Shirley Temple curls around her pretty face. My friend indeed looked like the most beautiful girl in the world.

Once I finished singing, the saxophone player started playing, and the leader of the band sang all jazz-like, "Happy birthday, baby. Happy birthday to you." Jabari twirled her in his arms, and Arianna threw her head back and laughed. Arianna and her husband looked very much in love and happy.

I was happy for them, and yet that voice popped in my head, saying, *This could have been you if you hadn't messed up.*

The scene before me, the beauty of it, had me misty-eyed. And what was more, the way her family and friends were looking at her . . . I don't know, I guess I wondered if the people that mattered to me the most would come out in crowds like that one day for my birthday. Would they have these happy, warm looks that were present that night? Or would it be disgust? Or pity, as though I'm so pathetic or screwed up? Would they even show up? I mean, I had my mother and my two closest friends by my side, but my sister acted like she still hated me and pretty much said that she did. She still had not reached out to me. I wondered if our relationship could ever be fixed.

I knew I had to think more positive despite how the situation looked. Being sentenced to life in prison and being paroled in five years taught me to always have hope, to see the light at the deep, deep end of the tunnel. So, I shook those thoughts out of my head and smiled and clapped for my friend.

I handed the microphone back to the band and I walked away. I sat down at one of the tables as the festivities continued. It started with a slide show from Arianna being a happy, bubbly baby to the age she is today. I was surprised to see pictures of both of us in some of the shots. There were pictures of her wedding and then her giving birth to her kids.

After the slide show, both her boys came out and presented their mother with roses. The food was then served. We ate the most tender filet mignon, lobster mashed potatoes, and asparagus. It all tasted good. Adults were served strawberry daiquiris as a cocktail, which was her favorite drink.

After we ate, her husband took the microphone and spoke. "I just want to take today to honor my beautiful wife. That one right there is definitely not one you see walking around every day. I honestly can say my life has true meaning now that she is in it. I honestly do not know what I would do without her. And she gave me the two greatest blessings: my twin boys." His eyes got all watery as he spoke, and a few women in the room said in unison, "Awwww."

"You made the ultimate sacrifice for me to have my career. You left yours to raise our sons. And no child on this earth could have had a better mother. So, to honor my beautiful wife, I got you a few things, baby."

Jaheim's "You Can Have Anything" was played by the DJ. The doors to the restaurant opened, and two restaurant staff wheeled a huge cart into the room with several beautifully wrapped boxes of different sizes. She was gifted with a Birkin bag, four pairs of Christian Louboutin heels, and a tennis bracelet. And this was all from her husband. She still had a table with plenty of gifts from guests that was piled high.

Arianna was loved for sure.

"Oh, y'all think that's something? Baby, you might as well move that ring to another finger." And damned if he didn't pull a small black velvet box out of his pocket. "Check that bad boy out."

Arianna screamed as he slipped her wedding ring off and placed another one on her finger. After admiring her new ring, she stood and kissed her husband.

"Thank you, baby!"

He kissed her back and patted her on her bottom. "Oh, you think I'm done? Baby girl, I'm just getting started. Follow me, everybody." He grabbed one of Arianna's hands and walked her outside.

We all followed them. And just like on an episode of *My Super Sweet 16*, there was a brand-new white Porsche truck with a pink bow on it.

"Baby, you're playing," she said, looking from the SUV to him.

He slipped the keys in her hand. That's all it took for my friend to go crazy, screaming and jumping up and down. Friends and family crowded around her and cheered. She opened the door and sat in the driver's seat. As she was looking around at the car, she put her arms on the wheel and pressed her horn by mistake. She tossed her head back and laughed.

The photographer had followed us outside and started taking more pictures.

We then went back inside, where people now took to the dance floor. While people danced, I went over to the dessert bar. I helped myself to a lemon cupcake. I bit into it and savored the flavor. It was very moist and sweet. I finished the cupcake and sampled a red velvet cake pop.

Someone grabbed me from behind in bear hug. It was Arianna. I chuckled.

She released me and said, "Alexis, I want you to meet someone. This is James, Jabari's friend. James, this is my bestie, Alexis."

I smiled, but when I saw the asshole from earlier who had cursed me out in the parking lot, that smile instantly dropped.

His smiled dropped as well when he recognized me. But he recovered quicker than I did and asked me, "How you doing?" He held out a hand for me to shake.

To not be rude, I shook it and said, "I'm fine, thanks." Then I politely turned away to say something to Arianna.

But before I could, someone whisked her away. "I'll be back, Alexis." She jerked her head in James's direction and winked.

Hell no, I thought. When I looked over my right shoulder at him, he just stood there staring at me like he was retarded or something. I turned my back on him and grabbed another cupcake.

"I don't think those thighs need any more yeast added to them."

I narrowed my eyes and turned around to face him. "What did you say?"

He chuckled, ignoring the question. "Hey, I've never seen you before, and I've been friends with Jabari for a while. Where are you from?"

"I haven't been around for a while. Not that it's really any of your business," I added.

"You had to throw that shit in, huh?"

"Do you have something to do?"

"Nope." To that, he started laughing. He had a glass in one of his hands, and it seemed that the alcohol mellowed his ass out.

I turned my back to him again, hoping he'd get it and walk far away from me. I waited a few seconds and looked over my shoulder.

He looked back at me, almost as if he were saying, "Yes, I'm still here."

I rolled my eyes and walked away, hoping he didn't follow.

I sat back down and watched Arianna and her husband doing karaoke, looking adorable. They were singing "My First Love." Although they sounded horrible, it was the cutest thing ever.

When they finished, James, the asshole, took the microphone. "This song dedicated to the cutie over there in the striped dress. Well, not because she a cutie. I've seen cuties before. I'm just faded right now." He pointed directly at me.

The crowd laughed and looked at me. I was embarrassed as hell.

When the music came on, he started jerking his hips and singing, "Cutie pie, you're the reason why. I love you so and never let you go." He was winking at me and smiling.

Jabari started whistling, and Arianna rocked to the beat while others sang along with him.

"You're the one who makes me feel so real. Hot! What a cutie pie."

I gave a fake smile, but inside I was seething. He was really grooving and having a good time at my expense. I should have knocked him out earlier. I didn't come to the party to be humiliated by some drunk buster.

When he finished his performance, someone thankfully took the microphone from his obnoxious ass. He pointed to me one last time before stumbling his ass away.

Arianna's mother stepped up to the mic and said, "Okay, everyone, please join me in wishing Arianna a happy birthday."

A server brought out a three-tier pink-and-silver chiffon cake covered in shiny diamonds. Everyone in the room started singing happy birthday to her, then the DJ Stevie Wonder version.

Arianna cried and said, "Thank you! I love you all!"

Yeah, Arianna was loved. Very well loved. Me, I was left feeling lonely and embarrassed.

Chapter 10

My alarm clock went off at six thirty. That gave me an hour to shower, get dressed, and see my parole agent. Over the past few months, she went from hating my guts to being indifferent. It was crazy. I couldn't explain it. I didn't trust it, that was for sure. I was certain one little mess-up and she'd have me back in lockup before I could scream boo. Maybe she was getting laid and that put her in a good mood. I know when I was getting good dick I was in a good mood. But whatever. As long as she left me alone, I was fine.

I lay in the bed, staring at the ceiling for a second. I noticed there was a funny smell in my room. I shifted in the bed and felt something cold and mushy on my body. It had seeped through my nightgown. I sniffed again.

No, it couldn't be. . . . I pulled the blanket back and screamed. There was shit all over me, my sheets, and blanket! It was on my arms, back, and legs. What the fuck was going on? Did I shit myself and not know it?

I pulled my sheets back and saw piece after piece smashed under my fitted sheet.

My mom, hearing me scream, came running in my room. Quickly, I pulled the blanket back over me.

"Alexis what's—" She paused and sniffed. "Lord, what is that smell?"

"I pooped on myself," I lied.

"Alexis, you mean to tell me that your grown ass shitted your pants?"

"I'm afraid so, Mom." I wanted her to get out of my room so I could get the shit off me. The smell was making me want to throw up.

My mom tried to remove the disgusted look off her face, but it seemed like she was having a hard time. "Do you need to—"

"Mom, just give me some privacy, please."

"Okay." As she walked to the door and proceeded to step out of the room, she continued casting looks my way with every step. "Oh, Jesus."

I got up quickly and rushed to the bathroom in my room. I turned on my shower super hot. As soon as the water heated up, I stepped in. I was in such a hurry that I fell in the tub. Feces smeared the tub as I struggled to get back to my feet. I grabbed my bar of soap and lathered up my body, but as I did this, my hands were touching the poop, which was making me feel nauseated again. My stomach suddenly lurched. I stepped out of the shower quickly and made it to the toilet just in time to hurl the contents of my stomach into the bowl. I stood there for a few seconds, waiting for my stomach to settle. Once it did, I flushed the toilet and stepped back into the shower.

As I scrubbed, I thought, *Without a doubt, the person who did this was Santana. But how was he able to get in the house? Maybe Mom forgot to set the alarm. Or maybe he snuck in while she was here.*

Who knew at this point? But what I did know was that neither I nor my mother was safe from him. I didn't want to be dishonest with my mother, but I didn't want her to worry. I was willing to take the embarrassment.

I scrubbed my skin until it felt raw, but there was nothing more disgusting to me than having shit of any kind on me. Damn, damn, damn that man was so fucking dirty. Droplets of water splashed the hot tears off my face. I lathered, rinsed, and repeated four more times until I was convinced I was clean and void of any poop. I stepped out of the shower and put on my robe.

I went into the pantry to grab a couple trash bags. I rushed back to my room and placed everything that was on my bed in the trash bags. I pulled both of them out of my room, down the hallway, and toward the laundry room, which would lead to the back door. I placed them in our dumpsters. When I stepped back into the house, I saw my mother in the living room, sitting on the couch, sipping a cup of coffee.

"I'm going to need a new mattress."

She remained silent as she sipped her coffee. I continued past her to get dressed to see my parole agent.

I ended up making it to the parole office a little late, which wasn't cool. As my punishment, she made me wait forty-five minutes in the lobby. I wasn't tripping, because she told me that would be a consequence if I were ever late. I'd rather wait in a lobby for forty-five minutes than have to spend years in a prison cell.

When she finally had me seated in front of her, I said, "Ms. Wilkes, I was wondering if I could talk to you about—"

She held up her left index finger. "One second. Let me finish typing this."

I chuckled nervously. "Okay."

While she was typing notes, her intercom buzzed, and the clerk who works the front desk connecting to the lobby said, "You have a visitor in the lobby."

She smiled and said, "I know who it is. Can you bring him back for me?"

"No problem."

She hung up the phone and turned back to me. "You don't mind if my boo comes in for a second, do you? He's bringing me lunch."

"No, not at all."

A few seconds later, when Santana waltzed into the interview room, all I could do was gasp.

"Hey, my hardworking woman." He leaned over and kissed her and eyed me quickly.

I looked down as my heart started to beat three hundred miles a minute. He handed her a Styrofoam container.

"Thanks so much for the food, babe!"

"Call me when you get off."

As he backed toward the door, he winked at me, but she was too busy blushing and taking a picture of the food to notice.

Once she finished typing and gave me my appointment slip, she asked, "Now, what did you want to talk to me about?"

"You know what?" I faked a laugh. "I forgot. I'll think of it and call you."

I signed my appointment slip, which wasn't an easy feat. Why? Well, because my hands were shaking and wouldn't stop. I dropped the pen two times, causing my parole agent to narrow her eyes at me. After signing, I jetted out of there.

I cried and punched the steering wheel in my car. I didn't know who to talk to. I was scared shitless. What the hell was his angle? It certainly couldn't be a coincidence. He must have been following me. But without a doubt, I knew he was plotting and trying to cause further damage. I wanted to talk to my mom about it but decided not to. Truth was, I wanted to ask my parole agent when she had started dating him. I assumed he was the reason she had been in such a good mood the last few months. If I was right and she had been seeing him since she was happy, I wanted to warn her about him and the danger he posed to her life. If it was new, I wanted to warn her that it was probably just to fuck with me. But I was scared it would all blow up in my face. What if she didn't believe me? What if he poisoned her mind against me and it caused more trouble for my life? Considering these factors truthfully, I didn't quite know what to do. She might not believe me, and it could just make things worse for me.

I went home, and to avoid blurting something out to my mom, I popped two Benadryl and went to sleep. I didn't even bother to eat dinner.

The next morning, my mother came in my room and woke me up. She hugged me and said, "I didn't hear a peep out of you yesterday when I came home. Then when I came and checked on you, you were knocked out, girl."

"I'm sorry, Mom. I wasn't feeling well."

"Well, I'm going to be leaving in about an hour for my Vegas trip. I sure wish you had asked your parole agent if you could come."

"It would have been a waste of time, Mom. I'm not allowed to leave the country, state, or even the county, for that matter."

She shook her head. "I know, but you never know. Maybe she would have made an exception."

"Hey, Mom, I was wondering if maybe I could in some way get back to working."

"That's going to be kinda hard for you with the felony on your record."

I chuckled. "Well, I was hoping maybe I could make a job for myself."

"Oh, how?"

"I really want to open up a restaurant."

"Oh, okay. Well, your father had an empty space over in Carson. He was planning on opening a fish market there. It's right over there off of Central. Baby, if that's what you want to do, then you know I will support it. Maricela has the set of keys at the office. You remember where her office is, right?"

How could I ever forget the location of my first real job? My dad had enough faith in me to let me run his properties. It was a huge boost of confidence for me. I thought it was the start of a lucrative career for myself. I was on my way to a life of comfort and fun.

From what my mother told, me Maricela took over when I left, and she had consistently been a trusted employee. Not long after I was sentenced, her husband lost his battle with cancer and passed away. Maricela continued to work for my parents and never faltered.

"Yes. I don't think I'd ever forget. It was my first job, and a job I never thought I'd be without."

"Let's not take the conversation in that direction. Go pick up the keys and check the place out. It has all the licenses, food permits, and everything. And it has a commercial kitchen there. What you would have to do is get your food handler's license. I was supposed to start the hiring process, but I've been procrastinating on it. From what I hear, it is fairly simple. You take the test online."

"Okay. Well, I will go check it out."

"All right, babe. Let me know what you decide." She leaned over and kissed me on my left cheek. "Gotta get going."

"Bye, Mom."

She left the room, and I stayed in bed, dreaming up a menu for my new restaurant. I'd think of a name after the menu was set.

Chapter 11

Two hours later, after leaving the bank, I found myself on South Street at my old office. So many memories came flooding back to me as I pulled into the parking lot, the worst being the fateful day Santana walked into the office. The day had started off like any other day. I got to the office, settled in, read emails, and began making plans for what I was going to do that night. I never anticipated I would be meeting someone who would dramatically change my life for the worse. If I could go back and change it, I would. I stepped out of my car took a deep breath to clear my head of the negative memory and walked up the stairs to the office.

I stepped inside and saw Maricela seated behind the desk that used to be mine. She was talking to someone on the phone. When she looked up and saw me in the doorway, it was like she had seen a ghost. Her face dropped, and all the color disappeared.

I motioned with my hand if it was okay for me to come in. With eyes wide, she nodded slowly, then she ended the phone call swiftly. For a moment, there was just silence. An uncomfortable silence.

"Hello, Alexis."

"Hi, Maricela. How are you?"

"Good, good. Thanks for asking." She was visibly thinner and her hair was now gray. She also had deep bags under her eyes. She stood. "Well, don't be shy. Give me a hug."

I chuckled and walked closer to her. When she held her arms open, I stepped into them, and she pulled me into a bear hug. The embrace felt sincere, not for show, and there was no awkwardness.

When we both pulled away from each other, she cupped my face between both of her hands and said, "I'd heard you were coming home. I'm so glad you're out."

I blushed and looked down at my shoes. "Thanks."

"You bet. Sit down, Alexis."

I sat in the chair across from her.

"It really is good to see you." She sounded really sincere, which was a relief. I wasn't sure how she would react to seeing me. I wasn't there to take her job, but I didn't know if that was what she would think.

"Thanks. How are your kids?"

"Oh gosh, they are well. They are taking their father's passing a lot better than I expected. Anna just graduated high school and is about to start college in the fall. Josiah and Jennifer, my twins, will be seniors in the fall. Both of them have over a 3.6 GPA. Ella is in junior high school and on the honor roll. And my youngest, Junior, is graduating sixth grade this year. I know if their father was alive, he would be so proud of them. I am so blessed to have such great children."

Now more than ever, those words I'd said five years ago—*I hope your husband dies*—were ringing in my ears and had me feeling like dirt. I cringed each time the words came to mind. Thing was, they wouldn't stop coming to mind. It was like they were ringing in my ears because Maricela was in front of me and that had been our last conversation before I lost my job.

I took a deep breath in hopes it would steady my shaky voice. "Maricela, I'm so sorry for your loss."

"Thanks, Alexis."

"When my father passed, he left my sister and me a trust fund. If it's all right with you, I'd like to give you this in hopes it could help, because I know you are doing this on your own." I pulled an envelope out of my purse and handed it to her.

She took the envelope and looked inside. When she saw the contents, her free hand went to her chest and covered her heart. She breathed deeply and said, "Alexis, what are you doing?"

Inside the envelope were four savings bonds, each totaling five grand for four of her kids. The bonds would mature when they each reached age eighteen. There was a check for her oldest daughter for ten grand. I wanted to give her a little cushion to start college with. She could use the money for books, school supplies, and anything else she needed for college. I'd also given a fifteen-thou-sand-dollar check to Maricela.

"I'm giving this to you and your family. I gave your oldest daughter a little more so she can prepare for col-lege. It's not much, but it's something to help you out."

Her lips trembled, and her eyes got watery.

"All my life, everything has been given to me. I never knew what it was like to have struggles until I created my own. Until I did time in prison. Honestly, I don't want anything from you other than for you to take the money. I just want to help. I used to be a very self-absorbed person. Everything was about me and what I wanted, and really, how anyone else felt just didn't matter to me. Well, I'm definitely not that person anymore. I thank God I had my crash moment to teach me what matters. Granted, I hate the messed-up choices I made and regret hurting the people I hurt, but I'm blessed for the lesson that came out of it.

"You are a good person, Maricela. You have always been. And your kids are lucky to have someone like you as their mother. You were taking care of a sick husband who any day could have been his last, yet you stood strong and did it all while raising the hell out of five kids. I don't remember ever hearing you complain. That takes a lot. My opinion is not much, but I really commend you."

Tears flowed and flowed from her eyes, and at one point during my conversation with her, she grabbed my hands in hers. "Thank you, Alexis. I really mean it. I always looked at your father as a friend. I never wanted to mess up your relationship. It was one that I always admired and wanted since I never had a father. So, I never ever wanted to come between you two."

I squeezed her hands. "Maricela, you did the right thing. I was wrong. I accept the responsibility for what happened. All of it."

We hugged again. I felt comfort and relief hearing Maricela forgive me. I shed tears of relief. We each cried into the other's shoulder.

I laughed and said, "I didn't mean to come here and make you all emotional while you're working."

"Oh, it's fine."

I nodded with a smile on my face. "I also came to get the keys to the restaurant over in Carson. I want to check it out, see what I could do to the place."

"Oh, what did you have in mind?"

I smiled. "You really wanna know? It's going to sound crazy, but here it goes. When I first got locked up at Twin Towers when I was fighting the case, I got this massive toothache. Turns out it was my wisdom teeth that needed to be pulled. At the dentist, I met this woman a few years older than I was named Cashmere. She had a cracked tooth from the officers that detained her. Anyhow, we got to talking, and she told me that she lived a life that was just horrible. She was abandoned, raped, forced into prostitution, had a husband who left her. She lost her daughters to the streets . . . to her old pimp. The girls' father."

Maricela's eyes widened. "What?"

"Yes. And she got locked up for killing him. In the midst of all of this, her first love came back into her life. She told me she worked for him in his bakery when she was only thirteen. How much more romantic can you get?

"Realizing the fact that my life was nowhere near as horrific as hers was, I felt like shit for how horribly entitled I was when I could have been Cashmere. But God had spared me. My parents provided a good life for my sister and me, so I should have never been in the situation I was in. I knew better.

"Meeting her had a way of humbling me. While we both fought our cases, we used to hang on the yard together. She taught me how to fight and everything. And all we ever talked about was food. Anyhow, I also got this idea to open up a restaurant of my own."

"That sounds like a great idea, Alexis. What will be your expertise?"

"Well, when I was in prison, the thing I craved the most was mac and cheese. And even though I was a cook at the facility in the last year, I was limited in what I could make. All I thought about was mac and cheese." I giggled. "So, I want that to be my specialty: different kinds of mac and cheese. Lobster mac, crab mac, and shrimp mac, and beef and potato so far are on my list."

"Sounds good. And that poor girl. Did you ever hear from her again?"

"No. But man, do I wish I had. I may try to find her on Facebook. So anyway, that's how I came up with the idea to try my luck at this restaurant. I've always been a good cook. I was even thinking if any of your kids wanted a part-time job . . ."

"Oh, Alexis, you are just so sweet!" She cupped my face between her hands and kissed both my cheeks.

I laughed. It was the least I could do for acting like such a bitch to her. I was selfish and jealous and not in my right mind.

We chatted for a few more minutes. I asked about her life now that she was a widow. She said she didn't have the desire to date and would probably stay alone. I was feeling the same way. Men had done nothing but ruin my life so far. My focus was on myself, not on hitching myself to some man who would only mess everything up for me.

She gave me the keys to the restaurant, we said our goodbyes, and I left the office. I drove over to the restaurant to take a look at it. It was located right by the 91 freeway off of Central and Artesia. It was actually perfect for what I wanted to do. Even though I eventually wanted to focus on mac and cheese, the best business decision for this location was a different kind of shop. I drove around the area to see what other businesses were there. It seemed that a cupcake shop was exactly what this area needed. There were donut shops galore, but no cupcake shops. A cute cupcake shop was going to do well; I could just feel it.

I drove to the Carson Civic Center, which wasn't far from the business, to get all the paperwork I needed to make this happen. I took it home to get started. It was exciting to begin this endeavor.

Time flew as I read over everything and started the paperwork. I was so engrossed in it that I lost track of time and would be late for Bible study. I grabbed my purse, keys, and phone, and locked up the house, making sure I set the alarm.

By the time I made it to the church, the main parking structure was packed to capacity. I had to park in the other structure across the street from the church. As I turned off the car and reached over to grab my purse, my door was yanked open, and I was pulled out by my hair. I fell to the ground and screamed.

A man with a ski mask loomed over me. He cocked one of his feet back, ready to boot-stomp me.

"Hey, what are you doing here?" a man screamed from across the parking lot.

The man and I both looked at James rushing our way. The man in the mask ran. James chased him but was unable to catch up to him. James stopped his pursuit and turned back to check on me. He reached over and pulled me to my feet. I wondered where security was. Since the lot was sort of secluded from the street, the church usually had a guard there for Bible study and church services.

"I don't need your help!" I lashed out angrily while snatching away from him.

"The hell? I just saved you from that crazy-looking man and that's what you say?" "Saving me doesn't change all the fucked-up stuff you said to me the other day, sooo," I snapped, brushing off my dress.

He nodded like he got it. "Well, I'm sorry. I been in a shitty mood as of late, and you were an opportunity to blow off some steam."

I tried to walk off, but he grabbed one of my arms firmly. "Wait. I'm calling the po-po for you. Damn!"

While we waited for the police, James apologized for his actions at the party. "Look, I'm sorry about the other night. I thought I was being charming."

"Well, you weren't. It was embarrassing and uncalled for," I said.

"I sometimes get stupid when I drink. I was intimidated by you, and I thought teasing you would be cute. I was trying to protect myself from getting hurt if I asked you out and you rejected me."

"That's a stupid way to act. Act like a man. If you wanted to ask me out, then you should get to know me, then ask for my number, not act a fool."

The police arrived and took a report. They said it would be hard to find the attacker because he was masked and there were no other distinguishing marks. How would he be able to be identified? I didn't need to see his face to know who it was. I broke down and told the officers I felt the person was Santana Marcelino. The officer notated everything and left.

James still stood near me, though. I rolled my eyes and walked away. He followed after me.

"I'm fine. Can you leave me alone now?"

"No. I'm making sure you get in this church safely. Blame the shit on my mother. She raised me right."

"Why are you here anyway?"

"Arianna and Jabari invited me. I didn't want to be bothered with the service, so I decided to come to the Bible study. Most churches make me laugh."

I ignored him.

Once we made it to the door, the ushers seated us, and since he was right behind me, he ended up sitting right next to me. The choir was in the middle of singing "I Got the Victory." Arianna was singing in the choir, and she looked like she was really enjoying herself. It made me want to be up there with her. I promised myself that I would join the choir when I felt the church had fully accepted me back. The thing I did notice was that the band was off. No one was in sync. Each instrument seemed to be playing a different tempo. The week earlier, they had been tight. The only difference was that the normal drummer was missing. It had shocked me the week before when I looked at the band and I recognized the drummer as the man who I'd seen fucking my sister. If it weren't for the strong voices of the choir, it would be all bad.

Our eldest deacon, Deacon Miller, didn't look too pleased. In fact, he continued to shake his head. On top of how bad the band sounded, the choir was also stalling because the pastor had not yet arrived at the church to start the service. They did announcements, which we usually only do on Sundays, and the choir started again. They had a couple kids come up and recite poems. Still, the pastor and the first lady didn't show. Then the choir resumed. At this point, an hour had passed, and still no sign of the them.

Finally, after another thirty more minutes of singing, they arrived. And although they had arrived, he came unprepared, and it was so obvious. He fumbled for his words, paused, and stammered. It was basically an incoherent sermon. It was all Deacon Miller could take before he exploded. I could see him getting more and more tense the longer the pastor went on.

He stood up and yelled, "Cut this shit right now!" He looked at Casey. "Boy, you let this church and congregation go straight to hell. Your father probably throwing up from his grave. Look at this place. Look how many people ain't bothered to come to Bible study. Since when is that okay? Goddamn band is all off. And where is the drummer? You come strolling your ass in here anytime you feel like it. This is the third time this month alone you been late! And this is all 'cause you got your head up her ass." The church gasped as he pointed at my sister, who was seated near the congregation

He then went in on her. "Don't look at me with those bubble eyes like you don't know what I'm talking about. You have got this entire congregation fooled, but not me, 'cause I see your tramp ass for what you really are! Hell, she sleeping with half the band. That's why they play like they don't give a good goddamn!"

I looked at James. His eyes were as wide as golf balls, along with the rest of the church. I felt like I was in the middle of a reality television show. It was unreal to watch a deacon shouting profanities in the middle of a church.

My sister jumped from her seat and ran off the stage. Deacon Miller calmly stood and walked off the stage. There was a moment of shocked silence throughout the church, until the choir director jumped up and directed the choir to start singing.

I left my seat and walked past the stage to the back to find my sister. I found her in the ladies' room. She was sitting in a stall, softly crying. I locked the door of the restroom so no one could enter.

I knocked on the door to the stall. "Hey, Bria. I know I'm the last person you want to see or much less talk to, but I came to check on you." I said the words quickly and held my breath, waiting for her to tell me to get the fuck out or call me out of my name.

But she surprised me by saying, "I don't know how to do this. All of this is a bit much for me! I'm trying to be a wife, a mother, and the first lady, and it's all just too much. For some reason, I feel like I'm going to fail. That's when I start doing stupid shit. Maybe I want to be caught so that I don't have to live this lie.

"Everything that Deacon Miller said is true. I am fucking the drummer. And I like it. I have never been good at being the good girl, Alexis. That's always been your job. Alexis, I have always been the fuck-up. My husband is the best thing that ever happened to me. He knows about my past, and still he pampers me. All I have to do is care for our baby and give him sex whenever he wants it. He treats me like a baby. And I love him for how he loves me, no questions asked, but when he leaves and takes our baby, I rebel. I cheat on him. I replaced my drug addiction with sex, and I'm so, so stupid to do this to such a loving man."

I couldn't believe she had opened up to me. It was what I had been praying for. I wished it was under better circumstances, but I would accept whatever God had planned for us. If this was how our relationship needed to be mended, then that is how I would handle it.

While it was a relief to know Bria had not fallen back into drug addiction, it was still disheartening to see she had replaced that addiction with another one. I really didn't know what to say to her. I was unprepared for the outpouring of emotion and trust she was placing in me.

But I was the older sister, and my younger sister was reaching out for help, so I was going to do the best I could. I took a deep breath and spoke from the heart.

"Okay. But now you're at a crossroads, and you have to decide. What do you want more?"

"What do you mean, what do I want more?"

"Do you want to continue to live on the wild side? Or do you want your family? Bria, you can't have both. One way or another, your other life is going to impede on the ones you love the most. If you want your husband, then you have to stop cheating on him. Take it from me. Addictions are never good."

I could hear her sniffling on the other side of the door. I heard her take some toilet tissue and wipe her face and blow her nose. She opened the bathroom stall and faced me. Her eyes were bloodshot, and mascara was staining her cheeks.

"Alexis, even if I decided to leave that mess, leave all the men alone, you saw what just happened. I'm humiliated. I can't ever show my face out there again."

I grabbed her by her shoulders. "You can and you will. If there is any place where you should be able to be redeemed, it's here in church. You know all about my scandal, all the things that happened, and here I am, back here seeking forgiveness. I'm not saying it's going to be easy, but you have to make the commitment. No one can do this but you, Bria. You may even need to go back into counseling. But know this: I will be with you the entire time. I'll support you and lift you up."

She nodded. "Alexis, I just want my family. My husband loves me, and I can't believe I am fucking that up!"

I nodded. "Well, let's fix it together, little sister."

Out of nowhere, my sister reached over and hugged me. She cradled into my shoulder and wept. I held her. My heart ached for her suffering. I wanted to take it all away for her.

"I'm sorry I said all those mean things to you. I just wanted you to see me. Growing up, I never felt you loved me. Arianna took my place as your sister. I just wanted you to see me. I wanted you to do things with me like you did with her." She started crying again.

"All these years, you were always the smart one, the one who made Mom and Daddy so proud, and they have always been disappointed in me. Dad was just good at not showing it like Mom did. Mom always showed it. And she is disappointed in me now too, Alexis. I hate myself for being such a fuck-up. No matter what, I was wrong for sleeping with Santana. *I just wanted you to see me.* And you only saw me when I did something bad.

"Alexis, I honestly didn't mean for it to go that far. I was so high out of my mind. But I knew what I was doing. It was wrong. And I don't hate you. I was angry you went to prison because it was another thing that took you away from me, but I shouldn't have been so childish. I should have been there for you. Maybe I thought with you away, Mom and Dad would start being proud of me. But I did nothing but marry and have a child. I was too lazy to even finish college."

Wow. I never knew Bria felt that way. I was used to being the only child, and my contribution to the sibling rivalry was my jealousy that I had to share the spotlight with her. My further distance was due to the fact that I just never approved of the choices she made and the grief she always seemed to cause my parents. And I also never felt Bria wanted a relationship with me. We were always so different. She is a Pisces and I'm a Gemini. Man, this was news. But at the same time, it made me feel good, because I now saw we had something to work and fight toward: a sisterly relationship. Man, if only Dad could have seen this.

"Bria, I'm sorry I wasn't the sister you needed me to be, believe me, but I would like to fix that. We can start over. I thank God we have this chance." I kissed her on one of her cheeks and she surprised the mess out of me by grabbing one of my hands and kissing it.

"I would very much like that, big sister." Then, as quickly as her smile came, it vanished, and her brows furrowed together. I assumed she was stressing about what happened a few minutes ago. The reality of what was to come and the work needed to get past this was setting in for her. In the past, she would have turned to drugs to quiet her fears and anxiety, but now she was going to have to rely on her own courage to make everything right. There was no avoiding the stress and work to come.

I tried to calm her fears. "Well, one thing your husband said at services last week is this: Darkness is temporary. We are always guaranteed a new day."

"Yes. He has an anointing, and I don't want to mess that up with my stupid decisions."

"That is the first step—admitting your faults and owning your decisions. Go get your husband. Take him home tonight and talk to him. Tell him the truth. He loves you."

"But he forgave me for cheating before. I don't know if he will this time."

"You have no control over how he reacts. You can only control you and your actions. It's better to stop the dishonesty altogether. Recommit to your husband. No more infidelity. Having a loving husband that puts up with it doesn't make it right. And if you need to go to counseling, Bria, I will support you."

She took a deep breath and put her head on my right shoulder. I leaned down and kissed her on her forehead. It seemed like the kiss comforted her.

There was a knock on the door. "Bria, are you in here? It's me." It was her husband.

I said, "Take your husband. Go home. I will address the church."

She nodded. Bria went out to face her husband. I heard them whispering on the other side of the bathroom door. I waited for them to leave before exiting the bathroom.

A few minutes later, I stood in front of the church. I waited until all the whispering quieted down before I spoke.

I ignored it all, even when someone said, "What are you doing up there, killer?"

Someone said, "Stop it and let her talk."

The congregation finally quieted down. I took a deep breath before speaking. "The pastor and the first lady left, but they will both be back on Sunday to address the church." I paused. "Look, right now the church is broken, just like some of us are broken on the inside. That's why a lot of us come to church: to fix what is broken. And some of us look to the wrong things to fix us to make us not so broken. Some of us do both. So then, now what? Do we throw them away? Outcast them? If the broken can't come here to heal, where are they supposed to go to heal? We have to look at how important our role is in a broken person's life.

"I remember coming to church to get my Word, to sing, and leaving feeling like I could conquer the world. In my journey of being a devoted Christian, I made a whole lot of mistakes. I disrespected the church and put the person that should have always been first last."

"Yeah, we know," someone yelled out.

I ignored it and kept going like it was never said.

"But the things is, I always remember this." I cleared my throat. "As the Bible says, we are renewed in the Word of Christ. In Christ, we are reborn. That is any sinner. That means any sin. Sounds crazy, right? But I didn't write it. If I had, I would have added this: take accountability for your mistakes. Own them, atone for them. Fully live in it. Then you move on, you rebuild. As some of us try to rebuild ourselves inside out, it's important that people who either haven't had to do the same or the ones that have remember it is our job to encourage, not turn them away. Pastor and the first lady have a love and commitment to this church, and I know they will get things back in order."

Suddenly, the church started clapping. Yes, there were a few that didn't, but the majority were on the same page. Or they pretended to be.

When it got silent, I said, "Now, I don't want to take up any more of your time."

"That's all right!" someone yelled.

"But I wanted to leave you a passage. It is in First Corinthians. *Therefore, judge nothing before the appointed time; wait until the Lord comes. He will bring to light what is hidden in darkness and will expose the motives of the heart. At that time, each will receive their praise from God."*

James' brows furrowed together, and he nodded. I didn't care much what he thought, but since he appeared to be so egotistical, if those three sentences could keep all the amusement off his face, then it had to have had some sort of value.

I jumped when people stood to their feet and started clapping for me. It was a perfect way to end the service. It was exhilarating.

After I exited the stage and walked down the aisle, a couple people even reached over and hugged me. I hugged back and made my way to the exit. I left the church, crossed the parking lot toward my car. I felt like I was floating. Standing in front of the people and delivering those words, hearing and feeling their response, was a moment I thought would never happen in my life. Sitting in prison all alone in despair, I could have never imagined getting the opportunity to preach to a congregation. It felt rejuvenating.

The rest of the church did what they normally do after Bible study; hung out and ate dinner. There were some parishioners who were only there for the food, that's for sure. But I wasn't going to judge them or fault them for that.

"Alexis."

I turned around and saw it was James walking up to me.

"That was good. You said the right thing after a massive fuck-up."

I chuckled. "Yeah, well, thanks." Despite the fact that I didn't want a compliment from him, it felt good to hear that I didn't look like a fool up there.

"I'm serious. Shit, I didn't know what you were going to say to calm them down. Damn. This sure was some service."

I laughed for a second and said, "Now, why are you following me?"

"Woman, just an hour ago someone had you hemmed up. Did you forget that?"

"No, I didn't." But damn, I sure did want to. I knew it had to be Santana. He was filling me with more and more dread, but I didn't know who to talk to. Maybe I could talk to Arianna's husband. Only thing was I didn't want to look like I had just got home and I was already in some bull. I made a mental note to bring it up to Arianna later, but I wasn't going to tell my mother.

We made it to my car, and I said, "Okay—"

"Get in your car. I'll follow you to make sure you make it home."

When I paused, he said, "You are stubborn as hell."

Since my sister was gone and my mother was a no-show, I would let him. Still, I didn't know if I wanted James to know where I lived.

"Get in your car. I don't want nothing from you but to see you home safely. 'Cause from what you told the cops, this seems like a train wreck kind of situation."

"The way you say stuff," I said sharply. "I bet you even make a compliment sound like an insult!"

He waved a hand and said, "Girl, if you don't—I want to get you home safely. Get in the car. Damn! You got a nut job in your life. Take it from me; that's a recipe for a fucking disaster."

I shook my head and got in the car as he ordered. He obviously wasn't going to take no for an answer. I put on my seat belt and started the ignition. I backed out and watched him follow me in my rearview mirror. Although he was an asshole, I did feel safer with him following me home. It seemed that Santana had been following me without my knowledge, so to have the security of James watching my back made me less stressed.

I pulled in, and he parked behind me in the driveway. I was surprised to see my sister's car. I would have thought she'd be at her home, working things out. My stomach filled with butterflies at the sight of her car. It didn't seem right that she was there.

James waited in his car until I made it inside before he drove away. I waved to him before entering the house. My sister was sitting on the couch when I entered.

Across from her was my mother, holding the baby and shaking her head at my sister with a disgusted look on her face.

"Hey!" my sister said. She looked so happy to see me.

"Hey, hey. Hey, Mom."

"Hey, Alexis."

I sat down next to Bria. She grabbed one of my hands and held onto it.

My mom looked at us, surprised, but kept quiet while patting the baby's back.

"So, what happened?" Bria asked.

"I told them to give you and your husband some time and you will address the church at the next service."

'How did they take it?"

"They seemed okay with it, Bria."

"I don't know if I ever will be able to face the church again."

"What do you mean, you don't know? Bria! When you made the choice to marry that man, you married the church. You are the first lady. You have to address the church. And your behavior has to come to heel," my mom said sharply.

Bria started crying. "I know, Mom. I know. I'm just so embarrassed after Deacon—"

"Spare me what the deacon said. I already know. My phone has been ringing off the hook since the service ended. I'm so glad I didn't go today. I would have lost it—on you and Deacon."

Bria turned to me. "Alexis, what do I do now?"

"First things first, you have to fire the drummer. There are plenty of churches around. He can work somewhere else. Number two, if you haven't admitted your infidelity to your husband, now would be the time, because when you address the church, you are going to have to show them that you two are a united force and he has forgiven you. Drummer should be out of sight and out of mind."

She looked down, took a deep breath, and said, "Okay. I think that's for the best."

My mom nodded. "Listen to your sister. If anyone knows how to come out of a storm, it would be Alexis."

"Have you talked to your husband?" I asked her.

"No. I started to, and I couldn't get the words out. I'm afraid to face him."

"Cut it out! Acting like this the first time you ran out on him—"

"I'm not saying that, Mom! Stop!" Her shoulders shook with sobs. "He forgave me last time. He just might not this time. I don't know what I would do if he left me."

"Well, that's the web you weave when you engage in that type of behavior," my mother said.

"Mom, you're always judging. That's why I can't talk to you. Why can't you support me for once?"

My mom shrugged as if she didn't care either way.

"I want to do right now. I swear I do. On the way over here, all I thought about was what if my husband really left me? The thought of it made me sick to my stomach. I don't want my daughter growing up in a broken home."

"Well, try to fix it," I urged.

"And if that doesn't work, then that's what you get, and next time, you will learn to sleep with your husband only," my mother snapped.

To that, Bria started bawling.

"Mom, that's not helpful right now," I said.

I squeezed Bria's hand and said, "Hey, don't cry. Remember, whatever will be will be, if it's meant to be."

The doorbell rang. I went to answer it. It was Bria's husband, Casey.

"Is my wife here?"

"Yes, she is." I stepped aside so he could enter. I closed the door behind him and followed him into the living room.

My mom stood to her feet. "Hello, Casey," she said.

"Hello."

"I'll leave you two." My mother took the baby and walked out of the room.

I turned on a heel to do the same, but I heard Bria plead, "No, Alexis, please stay."

I nodded and sat down across the room from them. I wanted to be there for my sister but to give them the space they needed to work it out on their own.

For a minute, Casey just stared at her. "Bria, all of this has to stop. You have to stop sleeping with the drummer."

She gasped and her eyes went wide.

"As much as I hate what you've been doing, it would—" He swallowed hard and cleared his throat. "It would—"

"It would what?"

He looked down.

"What?" she demanded, louder.

"Be the tea pot calling the kettle black."

"What does that mean?" she asked.

He took a deep breath. "I've been sleeping with the new choir singer."

Bria looked stunned. She didn't say anything or move for a few seconds. She simply stared at Casey. Then, she suddenly fell to the floor and sobbed loudly. She wailed and curled in a ball and continued to cry like a baby.

I heard a door slam. I knew it was my mother. She walked in the room, holding the baby, and looked down at Bria on the floor. "Bria, get off the floor. Stop it."

"No."

My mama handed the baby to me. "This is too much. I need a damn drink." She walked out of the living room.

Bria's husband knelt down in front of her and tried to calm her down.

I looked down at the baby's precious face. As she suckled on one of her tiny, tiny thumbs, I admired just how adorable she was and how very much she looked like my sister. Almost as if she were her twin. I wondered what it would be like to hold a baby of my own in my arms. The more I held this little angel, the more I realized I wanted to have one of my own. I hoped Bria wasn't just letting me hold the baby because she was distressed. I hoped we could work on having a relationship and that I could have a relationship with my little niece.

By the time I turned my attention back on my sister and her husband, Bria was now sitting on the couch, and her husband was sitting across from her. I sat down next to Bria. The baby had fallen asleep in my arms.

"What do you two want?" I asked the both of them.

"Well, I want my wife."

"Bria?" I looked at her.

"I don't know anymore, Alexis. I really don't."

"Well, you have to decide. I'm sorry you are hurting. You have had a rough day. And on top of what happened at church, you now know your husband cheated. But you both cheated. Bria, I also know you. If you were done, you wouldn't still be sitting there. What you two have to understand is that, well, playtime is over. You both have to keep in mind your vows. Surely you two didn't marry just to turn around and get divorced. If the both of you love this baby and each other, you have to at least to try to make this work. You both have to stop cheating on each other. You can say you'll stop now, but if you're not serious, you'll back-slide again. There is no other commitment more important than the commitment you two made to each other when you got married. And now there is a child involved. And in all actuality, neither one of you are in a position to be upset with each other, because truth be told, you both been running game on each other. But if you want this craziness to stop, both of you need to grow up and act like married people."

The entire time I talked, I was surprised to see my sister nodding her head as if taking it in.

"I know I screwed up, but I only did it because of what she was doing to me. I know it was wrong, but I was only doing tit-for-tat," Casey said.

Bria studied him as he spoke, and relief took over her face as he admitted the reason he had cheated on her. "So, you did this to get back at me?"

"Yes. And I'm sorry I did. So sorry."

"I'm so sorry, baby. I don't want a divorce either. I—" She swallowed hard. "I want my husband."

"Well, you got me, baby. I don't want anyone else to be the first lady but you."

"Okay."

"I will never cheat on you again."

She threw herself in his arms, and he held onto her.

My mother suddenly reappeared in the room. She took one look at them and started clapping sarcastically. "Okay, you two love each other and you don't want to get a divorce. Big damn deal. How about growing the hell up!" She pointed at Casey. "Hey, you with the ding-a-ling. Keep it in your pants unless you are using it on your wife." She pointed at Bria. "Hey, you with the hot twat. Keep your legs closed to rattlesnakes unless it belongs to your husband. I don't want to hear nothing else. You had me spend all that damn money on your wedding! For what? For y'all to make a mockery of marriage and the church? Hell no! Then on top of all of this, y'all have this beautiful child. She should come first. Not y'all perverted desires. If for nothing else, both of you should fall in line for her. You can both spare each other any further mess if you both not prepared to get it right!"

When they didn't respond, she snapped, "Bria!"

"I am, Mom. But why do you have to be so mean? Why couldn't you talk to me the way that Alexis talks to me, not bark at me, Mom ? You've done it my whole life. And you wonder why you can't ever get anywhere with me. That's why."

Now that was my mother's turn. Her moment of clarity, I guess, to self-check, to evaluate wrong on her part.

"Oh, so this is my fault?"

"No, Mom, but all my life, you have been so hard on me."

"That is because you were a bad-ass little girl. Always getting into stuff and always—"

"Always what? Say it, Mom. Always disappointing you."

My mom looked down at her hands and pulled her lips in.

"I know I'm a fuck-up, Mom. I didn't mean to be."

My daddy used to call my sister a free spirit because she was all over the place, and she had this crazy amount of energy that my parents tried to channel but just couldn't. She was just a preacher's kid, plain and simple, if you asked me. She enjoyed rebelling, and well, she just never grew to be the woman everyone now needed her to be. She probably thought she could continue to screw up and it wouldn't catch up with her.

"I'm sorry I didn't live up to your expectations. Maybe they were too high."

"So, me and your father giving you girls the best of everything and expecting you two to be successful ladies was wrong? Wow."

"Do you love me, Mom?"

My mom's face softened, and she said, "More than life, Bria."

"Then don't give up on me."

"I've never given up on either of you. Over the past five years, I know I have been emotionally out of it, but I thought my oldest child would never see her way out of that prison. So, for that, I am sorry, Bria. I am also sorry if I didn't make you feel loved. I always have loved you. You're my baby. I just wasn't too happy with the choices you were making over and over and over again. But it will never change how much I love you."

I watched my mom reach over and hug Bria. It changed everything about her body language.

"I hope we can all strengthen our relationships. Mom, Bria, we are essentially all that we have," I said.

My mom and Bria nodded.

Bria looked at me and gave this genuine smile.

All I could do was tell her, "I love you, Bria."

Her eyes twinkled and she said breathlessly, "I love you too, big sister."

Chapter 12

I watched as Bria took a deep breath and approached the podium with her husband by her side. You could hear a pin drop in the church. No was speaking; no one was moving. Everyone was transfixed by Casey and Bria.

Bria stepped up to the microphone and began, "The church is fragmented. Just as some of us are fragmented inside. And, church, I'm talking about me. I have failed the church and the congregation. I have shown you all what sin looks like. It looks like me, your first lady. I know my behavior has been disappointing at a time when I was supposed to be about bringing healing to my church family. I didn't realize that before I could bring the healing here, I needed to bring the healing to myself.

"Everything that happened during Bible study was a blessing in disguise, believe it or not. It opened the doors for conversations that were long overdue. Conversations that cleaned old wounds. It brought about forgiveness, gave clarity." Tears streamed down her face as she spoke, causing some women in the church to follow suit with their tears.

"I want to tell the church how sorry I am for letting you down, and I ask that you give my husband and me another chance to rebuild as we are working on rebuilding ourselves and our marriage. One thing you don't have to worry about is us ever letting the church down

again. We are more committed than any of you will ever
know. Second Corinthians 5:20 says, *Now then we are
ambassadors for Christ, as though God did beseech you
by us: we pray you in Christ's stead, be ye reconciled to
God.* Even me. I'm holding on to this, because I want to
be a blessing to someone else. I'm here with a job to do,
and I plan to take that job more seriously."

There was a pause after she finished, then the congregation applauded, which surprised my sister. I don't
think she had expected them to applaud her or to accept
her back.

Before the service, we'd had a pep talk, and I helped
her write her address to the church. They decided that
they would get baptized during the service to show
that they were recommitting to the church. The congregation was really moved by what they saw, and my sister looked on in amazement that they appeared to have
forgiven her. What didn't hurt was the fact that Bria and
her husband had fired the drummer and gotten rid of the
choir girl.

It was incredible to watch how quickly the new drummer learned all the songs. They definitely did their
clean-up work swiftly and didn't miss a beat for church
service.

After the service, we went to my mother's house for
Sunday dinner. While my mother prepared dinner, Bria,
her baby, Justin, and I all sat in the living room. And
finally, things felt right.

I was holding the baby, and Bria and I were chatting
it up like we had been close for years and years. And the
crazy thing was it seemed real. Genuine.

"Thank you again, Alexis."

"No problem. You cleaned up things really well. You
and Casey."

"Do you think the church will really get over it and forgive us?"

"If they can forget my scandal and accept me, anything is possible," Justin said.

"And if they can get over mine—" Before I could finish, we all started laughing.

"Well, you're not done, big sister, and I'm not done with you. I want more!"

I looked at her, confused.

"I want spa dates. I want you to come over and cook for me. I want to call you and vent when my hubby gets on my nerves. I want you to come get the baby when I need a break. . . . I want my sister."

"And you got me, little sister. I ain't going nowhere anymore." Well, I hoped I wouldn't. If I did, it would be by force.

Just then, my phone rattled on the coffee table, making the baby stir. Justin leaned over and handed it to me. It was a text from Arianna: Taco Tuesday at The French Quarter. See you there. No backing out.

I chuckled and set the phone down next to me.

The baby went from stirring to being fussy to full out bawling.

"She's hungry," Bria said.

Justin stood to give her privacy to breastfeed, but she said, "No, Justin, stay. I can always go in one of the bedrooms."

Justin sat back down as Bria gently scooped her baby out of my arms and left the living room.

"I have never seen her so . . . unselfish," Justin said, shaking his head.

I chuckled and said, "Shut up."

"Truth." He studied my face. "What's going on with you, bestie? And don't say nothing."

I debated whether I should tell him. Whether smart or not, I needed to not just confide in someone, but I needed it off my chest, and I knew I could trust Justin. I had to speak on this because it was tearing me apart, keeping me up at night and giving me straight diarrhea. I had to run to the bathroom twice during church service. How embarrassing.

"Follow me to the front porch."

Once we made it there, I took and deep breath and confessed what had been going on with Santana.

Justin was quiet for a moment before saying, "Crazy."

"I know, right? Why won't he leave me alone?"

"No, not him. You. I wouldn't put anything past that lunatic. But you, baby girl, you need to take action, and I don't know why the hell you haven't."

I explained how I went to the police, but without an address, he couldn't be served.

"Your other best friend is married to a supervising district attorney. Why haven't you went to her? I'll wait."

"I don't know. Embarrassed, I guess. To just get out of prison and already be caught up in this mess."

"But it is not of your doing. The man is crazy. Bring it up to Arianna and see what she thinks. Remember, the past is in the past. We're on your side now. You can't be scared to speak up."

"Well, she did invite me to Taco Tuesday. Maybe I could bring it up there."

"You better, because I will be calling her to make sure that you did. So, you have no choice."

I chuckled despite the severity of the situation.

When I arrived at The French Quarter, all the tables were taken. The bar, however, had plenty of space.

Arianna was running late. I sat at one of the stools at the bar and set my purse down next to me. I thought about how I would tell Arianna. I was worried that she would be turned off by the fact that I was asking her and possibly her husband for help. Just then, my stomach grumbled, indicating I had to use the restroom . . . yet again.

I grabbed my purse and raced there quickly. I passed by a woman in front of the mirror, lining her lips. I made it just in time, and as I felt my insides about to erupt, I placed a seat cover on the toilet seat and sat down. I moaned and closed my eyes as I relieved myself.

"What the fuck?" someone yelled. Heels clattered on the floor, and the bathroom door opened. As it slammed shut, she yelled, "Stanky bitch!"

I ignored her, although embarrassed.

"This has to stop," I said to myself. It reminded me of the first three months being locked up. I couldn't stop using the bathroom. That was my anxiety kicking back in because of Santana.

I stepped back out, washed my hands, and dried them. I moved slowly just in case I had to use the restroom again, but it seemed I was okay. I searched in my purse as I made my way back to the bar for an Imodium AD. Luckily, I had one left.

When I made it back outside, my seats were occupied. The bar had filled up quickly. I looked around and didn't see any more vacant seats. I pulled my phone out to see if Arianna had texted me or called. She hadn't. As I tried to place my phone back in my purse, I felt someone bump into me from behind.

Being at a club, although annoying, this was typical, so I ignored it until I heard, "Are you just going to stand in the damn way?"

I ignored that comment also and stepped to the side. My reason for ignoring was different this time. Before, it was out of fear; now . . . well, there was no more fear of a female in me. That fear had washed away years ago after being punked so many times until I decided to stand up for myself. I only fought if I absolutely had to, and I refused to fight because a dumb broad bumped into me and was mouthing off. The ball game was different now. I was on parole and could easily go back. I wanted no problems either way. I had a specific condition that prevented me from engaging in criminal conduct.

Although people around me laughed, I perceived the laugh due to the fact that I didn't respond. Still, I ignored the laughs and comments. Whatever. But then, that didn't seem to be enough for the person, who I still hadn't looked at.

She made it a point to bump into me again, although now there was plenty space for her to get by.

"Can you please—"

In a flash, she was in my face. "Please what, bitch?"

I took a deep breath, and before I could exhale, wetness covered my eyelids, nose, and cheek. She had spit on me. Before I could stop myself, I took off and hit her in the face with two closed fists.

"Bitch!" She swung on me.

I backed up and leaned in with my fists and drilled her with two left hooks. I ended up getting the best of her, until I felt the pressure of a fist from behind hitting me in the back of my head. I was getting jumped.

Thinking quick, I grabbed the hair of the girl in front of me and backed the other girl into the bar. I then swung the other girl by her hair with all my might, until she flew a few feet away. I then turned around quickly and started throwing hands with the other girl.

From the corner of my eye, I saw the other recover, rush back to her feet, and come toward me with a bottle in her hand. I took my phone and busted her in the face with it, making a loud cracking sound. My hand and phone were now covered in blood. The girl screamed at the top of her lungs at the blood that covered her face. At that point, she didn't get up.

The other girl came for me again. I shoved her with all my strength, thinking that the police would be called, and if I kept going, they would arrest me. So, I turned and ran out of that place.

My heart pounded loudly in my chest as I ran. The last thing I needed was to get a new arrest, but damn, the girl kept pushing it. I wished I had just wiped the spit off my face and walked away. Then I wouldn't be in this fear of getting locked up again.

As I ran through the parking structure, I bumped head on into a broad chest.

"Damn, that's how you greet people?"

I looked up at James's amazed face. When he spotted the blood on me, he asked, "Are you okay?"

I ignored him and raced to my car as he chased behind me, saying, "What's going on with you now?"

To my surprise, when I got to my car, I saw one of my tires was on flat. "Fuck!"

"What's wrong? Can I help?"

"Yes. Can you get me out of here now?"

Twenty minutes later, I was in the bathroom of James's house, scrubbing my phone and hands free of the girl's blood. Once clean, I lathered my hands and arms with sanitizer, all the while thinking of the mess. Why would those women just mess with a stranger who didn't want it? For the sake of messing with someone just because? Man, I sure hoped the police weren't called. I took a deep breath and walked out of the bathroom.

"James?" I called.

He poked his head through a sliding door. "Come out here."

I walked toward the balcony and paused in the entry-way. He was sipping from a tumbler glass. I stepped out completely and walked toward him.

I sat next to him, and he handed me a glass.

"You need this. It's Henny"

"Thanks." I took a small swig of the strong liquid and coughed. Despite the struggle to take it down, I tried because I knew he was right—the night was crazy.

"Okay. My mechanic located your car. He towed it to his shop. He's going to fix the flat and have it towed to your house."

"Thanks. Did he say if police were there when he towed my car?"

"No. He needs your address."

He handed me his phone, and I texted my address to the mechanic and handed it back to him. I hoped to God things really were that simple an no one had called the police.

"So, can you tell me now what that was about?"

"I honestly can't tell you what I don't know. A lady bumped into me two times and spit in my face. I lost control of my temper, and then another jumped in, and they both tried to jump me."

"So, what did you do?"

"What do you mean, what did I do? I beat their ass."

He threw back his head and laughed. "All right then, slugger." His Southern drawl was evident when he said this.

"But what were you doing there?" I asked.

"What do you mean, what was I doing there? Shit, I can't be in Bellflower?"

"No, that's not what I meant." This man had such a smart-ass mouth. I'm glad I wasn't in my prissy days. The old me would have dismissed him whether he helped me or not.

"Jabari invited me to hang out. Said they had good po boys. Only I left with you. I called him while you were in the bathroom, and he didn't know anything about it, which is weird as hell, because he texted me on Sunday and told me to meet him up there for Taco Tuesday. But since I had this going on with you, I didn't ask any further questions. I wanted to know what in the hell you had going on with you all running out of there like a bat out of hell. So, I told him I'd call him back."

That's when it hit me. I threw my head back and laughed. "Now it makes sense. Arianna set us both up."

"What do you mean?"

"What time did she tell you to meet up there?"

"Well, like I said, Jabari texted me. And he said six."

"I don't think he texted you. She did. Seems like someone is secretly trying to play matchmaker."

"Well, hell, I don't have a woman, so I'm all for it."

"For what?"

"Us fucking. I can't see myself being able to give anything else," he said bluntly. One of his hands draped around my shoulders. If this man only knew.

I gently slid from underneath his arm and stood to my feet. I walked to the edge of the balcony and looked at the view of the beach.

"You don't even know me, and you just so easily—"

"You can't be all *that* bad. I mean, I know you just assaulted two women. Your sister is banging all the band, but hell, that's gangsta in my book."

I looked back at him and chuckled while he eyed me up and down.

"I mean, what's the worst thing you did? It can't be all that bad. You haven't killed anyone, right?" Then he took a swig from his glass.

I locked eyes with him and arched a brow. "Yes. Yes, I have."

To that, brown liquid spewed from his mouth. That's when I started laughing.

"Damn! I guess you really can't tell a person by their looks. Just 'cause you're fine as hell."

"Whatever."

"So, what happened?"

I told him the story about what happened the night I killed the officer by accident.

Afterward, he said, "Oh. That was an accident."

"Well, there is more to the story."

"Go on."

"The person I was sleeping with, in love with . . . was actually my brother."

James started coughing loudly. I shook my head and waited for the judgment or questions.

"Willingly?"

"No. I didn't know. He knew. It was a plot. Revenge on my mother for giving him up for adoption. Long story short, I ended up serving five years in prison, and it was there that I found out the truth about him. During the time I was with Santana, I was reckless, selfish, and self-centered. I didn't care about anyone else at all. My behavior was disrespectful to how I was raised and plain out of control. I hurt all the people around me that mattered. While I was locked up,"—I swallowed hard—"my father passed away." My eyes watered, thinking about my dad.

"Wow. I mean, you do get the fucked up family award."

I chuckled.

Then he turned serious. "Have you forgiven yourself yet?"

It was funny that he asked me that, like he was reading my mind and saw all the inner conflict there with what I had done five years ago.

"I been trying to for the longest. Although the people around me have. My friends, my family, even my church seems to be coming around, but I just can't seem to. I really don't think you would understand."

To that, he tossed his head back and laughed. "Listen, about seven and a half years ago, I met the woman of my *dreams*. Pretty, smart, ambitious, humble, and as sweet as peach cobbler. And she had a beautiful little mini-me with puff balls running around. Being around them was a sweet overload on a daily basis. Allure and Sierra." He chuckled. "But when I had them, I didn't do right by them. I left Allure when she got pregnant by me.

"Then I felt threatened when she didn't chase after me. I'll admit, my family comes from money, so it made me a little arrogant. It was like I was thinking, 'How dare she not chase after me? I'm the catch. I'm better than her because my family has money, I'm educated, and have a career.'

"And seeing her talk to another man had me hot and scared. So, I asked for another chance. She gave it to me. Then I cheated on her." He laughed again.

"How Allure found out was a trip. She, seven months pregnant and all, climbed in the back of my truck without my knowing. And my dumb ass went to pick the girl Latonya up, and right when I'm about to do dirt, wham! Allure jumps out the back of the truck. I'll never forget the look of pain on her face. And after all of this, still this woman gave me another chance.

"We had a beautiful baby boy named Jeremiah. Now, finally I felt like I had a real purpose in my life. Money, plenty of women, accolades . . . nothing ever amounted to how that baby made me feel. But . . ." He cleared his throat.

"He died out the blue of SIDS. And that pain of losing my first born was something I couldn't recover from. I made a decision: instead of grieving, I would blame. It was easier. And I blamed Allure. One day, I treated her so bad, I'd be unable to ever speak on what I did to her. And then I left her. Got the girl I cheated on her with pregnant.

"So, I tried to do what was right in that moment and marry Latonya. This part is going to make you think I'm a major dick," he warned. "The day of my wedding, early that morning, I don't know what I was thinking, but I showed up on Allure's doorstep. She let me in, and I made love to her. And although I was supposed to get married to Latonya, I swear I didn't wanna leave. But I did, and I never came back, and Allure ended up finding out through my brother that I had gotten married. Latonya, my ex-wife, professionally had triple what Allure had, but still somehow, Allure managed to be triple the woman Latonya was."

"Why did you divorce?"

"Latonya gave me two beautiful sons, but there wasn't much I could give her, because I didn't love her. And for her, that was everything. So, not giving her that one thing killed her. Thing was, I have always loved Allure. She knew. And four years ago, instead of accepting the bed I made for myself and trying to be the best husband I could, I couldn't get over my obsession with Allure. So, I sought Allure out again. At this point, she had graduated from college, worked as a school teacher, and bought a house. Sierra was beautiful and doing well. And there I go, confusing things.

"Long story short, I was willing to divorce my wife and marry Allure, but a combination of things happened. My wife went stone cold crazy, tried to kill my kids and Allure and herself."

I gasped.

"But the only life that ended up being taken was her own. Allure survived her gunshot, and my kids were unharmed."

"So, there was your chance to finally be with Allure, right?

"Allure married someone else. She never took me back. I lost her. She is now happily married and has three kids."

"And you?"

"I am raising my sons and trying my best on a daily basis not to sit in anguish over the fucked-up decisions *I* made. Because, albeit corny, I have never found anyone to make me feel the way that woman did. Cold part: she was mine, all mine, and I just gave her away. I arrogantly thought she'd always be there for the taking and timing of my choice, and that she would always come back to me. Then, I thought, *okay, James, you going to have to do some work to get her back, but you can get her back. The fuck? Remember who you are. The alpha male. That nigga. The one*. But then, harsh reality hit me that she just didn't belong to me anymore.

"And I have to accept this. And hell, for the longest, I couldn't. That's the thing about life. Well, life for me, anyway, is accepting a fate you just don't want to. Not accepting it had me depressed. Eventually accepting it had me depressed. There really was no safe haven, no resolution for me.

"The analogy I like to use is having an investment opportunity. Stock is at an all-time low, and you pass on the chance to buy any because you don't see the value in it. Then it shoots to billions.

"So, Miss Alexis, I guess you can say someone understands. This dumb Negro here. You know how many times I replayed different events that happened when we were together? And in the end, it got me nowhere, because the reality was the same. I had lost her."

"And you've never met anyone since her?"

"Yes. I'm a man. I like to fuck. But even that took a minute to even build my dick up to put it in another woman. I have slept around, but developing feelings for another woman? Nope. She will always be the standard."

Wow. That was crazy. I didn't know what to say.

His eyes even got watery.

I held one of his hands and said, "Have you forgiven *yourself?*"

He shook his head.

"Is there anything I can do to help you, since you helped me?"

"No."

Chapter 13

After James dropped me off, I called Arianna. She didn't answer. I left her a voicemail, telling her to call me. It was pretty slick of her to call herself doing match-making for me, but I knew she meant no harm. When we did talk, I would make sure to let her know that right now was just not a good time for her to be trying to play matchmaker. I had to get my life in order first, and the presiding issue was Santana. He had to be stopped one way or another before things got out of control. Then, I wanted to get the restaurant together.

To be honest, after spending the night getting to know James, I'd decided he wasn't so bad. He had a lot of barriers up to protect himself, but I understood. I felt the same way. Once you got past his defenses, he was funny and sweet. Dare I say, he was sensitive, although I was sure he would hate for me to describe him like that. Even with all of his good qualities, I wasn't ready to seriously date anyone. Yes, I was horny as hell. There was only so much masturbating a person could do! But I just didn't want the involvement. But damn . . . James sure was fine.

I shook the thoughts out of my head and settled down in my bed. My phone went off, telling me I had text messages. The first was from my sister, asking me to go with her and the baby to take pictures and out to lunch, and then to babysit so she and her husband could go see a movie. I chuckled, thinking she was going to pretty much take up my whole day. But that was fine. I could go over to the restaurant around 6 a.m. and work there for a few hours before going over to my sister's.

I expected the next text to be from Arianna, but it was James instead saying hi. I didn't respond.

The next text was from a different number I didn't recognize. It read: Did you enjoy that ass whipping trick? There are more coming your way.

My heart started pounding, and I blocked the number. Now it made sense why those two women had jumped me. He had set me up yet again and probably was the one who messed with my car. Damn. I shook my head and dialed Arianna again, but still no answer. This wasn't the time she needed to be ignoring me. I needed help. I didn't know how much torture I would be able to take from Santana. I needed a plan to put an end to his terror. My mind raced and raced as anxiety filled me and caused my shoulders to tense up. Why couldn't this man just leave me alone?

All night, his words rang out in my head, keeping me awake. I got up and popped two Benadryl so I could go to sleep. Before I dozed off, I thought, *Damn, I wish I knew what more he had coming my way.*

***

The next day, I did as promised and went over to the restaurant with Maricela's kids to paint. I chose a silvery blue and dark chocolate color scheme. It looked better than I had envisioned. As I painted, James continued to text me. When I wouldn't respond, he started calling.

I laughed, shook my head, and responded with a text.
Hey, James.
Oh, now you're speaking.

LOL. Been busy.

OK. Well, I was just checking on you.

Thanks, that's nice of you.

No problem. I mean, it did take a minute for your ass to respond. I guess you thought if you didn't respond I was going to stop texting. Nope. And then if you didn't want me to hit you up you would have had to tell me why.

Why would I have had to?

Because I'm an alpha male and I would have drove you crazy.

I chuckled.

What you have going on?

Painting.

Painting what?

My family owns a commercial space. I'm going to turn it into a little restaurant.

Cool, Ms. Entrepreneur.

Thanks.

All right well, just checking on you. Hit me up later when you have the chance, because you did ask if there was anything you could do.

I chuckled. *Oh, Lord.*

Will do.

I thought maybe it wasn't such a bad idea to talk to him. I mean, he seemed harmless, and no one else was giving me any attention at that moment.

When I made it to my sister's house, she came running out with her husband right behind her, with the baby in one arm and the diaper bag in the other. She pulled the passenger door open and excitedly sat down. She threw herself in my arms.

"Hey, sister!"

I hugged her back and said just as cheerfully, "Hey, little sis!"

My God. It felt more genuine than ever. We really were mending our relationship.

"Hey, Alexis," Casey said as he opened the rear door.

"Hey now, Pastor. Working on a good Sunday sermon?"

"Sure am."

I stared at my beautiful niece. Nya looked so adorable in her pink dress with matching headband.

He secured the baby in the car seat, kissed her, set the diaper bag next to her, and closed the passenger door. He then came around to the front of the car, opened the car door on Bria's side, and kissed her.

"You ladies enjoy."

"Thanks," we both said in unison.

She looked at me, and her brows furrowed. "What's wrong? You sound happy, but you *don't* look happy."

The last thing I had planned to do was scare Bria with talk of that motherfucker. I wanted to deal with it myself and not involve my family. He had put them through enough.

"You know I always had the resting bitch face."

To that, she laughed.

"Sometimes you have to deal with these trifling bitches in the world." Then, her slender fingers covered her mouth. "I'm a first lady. I know better."

"You can't be perfect."

She looked at me and nodded. "Alexis, I just might always be a little wicked."

I laughed. "With limits, I hope, missy."

"That's why I got you to keep me in line and remind me of those limits. I know we had our problems in the past, but I'm so willing now to heed any advice and guidance you have to give."

Wow, more touching words from my sister. My heart was filling with so much love for her.

"You are doing a good job."

"Thanks. Means a lot coming from you."

"Awwww."

She turned on the radio. Big Sean's "Bounce Back" was playing. My sister started dancing.

"Let go," she said, sounding like a rapper.

I laughed, started the ignition, and pulled out of her driveway.

We ended up taking Nya to Olan Mills to take her pictures. The experience was the funniest. Nya was just so adorable, and I had to admit my sister seemed like a great mom the way she was able to get her daughter to perk up and smile for the camera lady.

After the pictures, we went over to the Kickin' Crab, which I didn't mind, in Buena to have a messy lunch of Cajun fries, garlic noodles, king crab, lobster, and shrimp in their kickin' sauce. Oh, so good! What was cute about when we were sitting was how my sister's nose keep running. That had been going since she was a little girl. The food didn't have to be hot, but anything with spices did that to her, from tacos to chili to spaghetti. I laughed and grabbed a napkin and wiped it off her face so she could keep attacking the massive crab leg she had in her little hands. We talked about so much, from music to making plans to get Beyoncé concert tickets to going to a twerking class to bedroom secrets.

"Alexis. I have to know this."

"Shoot, girlie."

"How were you able to last in that place without getting some meat stick?"

I laughed. "Meat stick?"

"Well, it's better than me saying dick."

"Watch it, First Lady."

She threw back her head and laughed. "Sorry. I just don't know how you were able to do it."

"I had no choice. And pretty often, I was so down about my predicament I didn't worry about sex, to be honest."

"Yeah, but you can't say that now," she countered.

I smiled. Yes, I was horny. I dealt with it by using my fingers.

She watched me. "Aww, come on. Tell me you got some."

"No. I cannot say that I have."

"What?"

The baby jumped in the car seat.

"This must stop!"

"*This* must stop. You're a mess." I laughed until tears came out of my eyes.

"I'm saying you have been locked down, sexually oppressed. Ordinarily, in our life group, I teach the women young and old to wait until marriage, but in this situation, sister, God will understand!"

More laughs came out of me until my face was sore.

"Are you seeing anyone?"

"No, but Arianna tried to play sneak matchmaker and set me up with one of Jabari's friends."

"How is he?"

"Okay. Bit of an alpha male slash asshole."

"*Girlllll,* they be the ones to tear you up in bed."

"Again, First Lady."

She laughed and placed both hands in the air.

"I don't know. We kind of connected, but my head is nowhere near."

"Alexis, if you don't get broke off and repent later!"

"You really not going to stop, are you?"

She winked. "Probably not. You probably gonna need some coaching it's been so damn long."

I almost fell out of my chair at that.

The conversation took a somber turn when she said, "It's okay if you don't want to talk about it, but I have to know. How did you get that hideous scar on your neck?"

I had lost my celly. Cashmere was transferred out, and I was bunking alone. My cure for my loneliness was singing. I sang during rec for women on the yard. Out of boredom one night, I signed up for the holiday talent Show. The winner of the concert would win a fifty-dollar gift card to the canteen. I didn't care about winning. I just needed something to do to occupy my time that day. There was a long list of women participating. Some were singing, some were rapping or dancing routines, and some were doing acting skits. The most entertaining one was Whoosie and her cellie, who acted out a scene from the movie Set It Off *when Cleo got killed by the officers. I thought for sure she was going to win, but when I belted out "Here I Am" by Tamela Mann, I received a standing ovation. Even the prison guards were impressed.*

I didn't even keep the gift card. What I did instead was give it to Whoosie. All things considered, even though we had fought and she had bullied me at one point, I never saw her able to buy anything from the canteen. I was trying to make peace and show that we could get along behind bars without fighting each other. I was hoping to be an example for the rest of the women behind bars.

That's why it was always a shock to me that when lights were out, I woke up to find someone leaning over me with her upper body so I couldn't move. And what was more scary than that was the fact that she had a shank to my throat. And it was her. Whoosie. Somehow, she sneaked in my cell. I think she must have bribed a guard. Who knows what she had to give him to be able to get in my cell.

With the shank pressing against my throat, she said, "Don't move, bitch."

I froze out of fear. I pleaded with my eyes, but she stared down at me hatefully.

"Bitch, you will never be able to sing again." In a swift motion, she swiped my neck as the sharp blade sliced through my flesh.

I used my upper body strength to throw her off me. I did not want to die in that moment. I gripped a hand over the shank and managed to pull it away before she could cut me anymore. As blood streamed down my neck, I fought her off until she fell off the bed and onto the floor. As she escaped out of my cell, I stumbled out as well with one hand over my neck and the other flagging a guard down before I collapsed in a pool of my own blood.

I looked at Bria's shocked face.

"It's crazy you survived that."

"Had I not kept a hand over my neck, I wouldn't have."

"So, you mean to tell me the bitch wanted to kill you because you could sing? Out of jealousy?"

I nodded.

"What a crazy bitch! Man, you are a true champ to have went through all of that and still be here. I admire you!"

I never thought I'd hear my sister say those words to me. It made me feel good.

"I'm so glad you survived that shit. What happened to her?"

"She was sentenced to more time and shipped to another prison."

"Wow. Crazy. I don't even know what to say. To think I could have lost you . . . Well, just know that's over now, sister. You're home."

"Thanks, little sis."

My sister changed the subject, which I was glad for, because I didn't want to think of that day anymore anyway. As she continued to talk, all I thought about was how much fun the sister date was and how grateful I was to be home free and able to spend time with my sister. We really had a good time together. We joked, laughed nonstop, had girl talk and everything. I lived for more days like those.

The highlight of the night was being able to babysit my precious niece while Bria and her hubby enjoyed date night. I helped her get away, and I was able to bond with the baby. She was so precious and such a good baby. Being in her presence . . . words couldn't describe having the ability to be able to watch her on my lonesome. The fact that my sister trusted me, despite my mother's words—"Be careful with Bria. She is the type that will leave her baby with you and forget she has a damn kid. You have to put out a SOS for her to come back."

But I didn't care if she was late coming back. I really was enjoying the time with the baby. We sat and watched cartoons. She was so fascinated with all the colors. I fed her and changed her diaper, which didn't go so well. As I was cleaning her and reaching for a clean diaper, she decided to poo all over the changing table. I'd never seen such a mess.

I played music off my phone and even sang to her. She loved it. She cooed and smiled, showing all her little gums. The way it felt, I really couldn't describe the joy it was to be able to hold her, feel her soft skin, smell her sweet smells, and yes! Feeling the success of finally getting her to burp. I also enjoyed her sweet breath against my cheek as I rocked her. Man, I was being blessed. God was blessing me in so many ways, and I saw it, felt it, and appreciated it.

After Nya went to bed, I had plenty of time to sit with my thoughts. I couldn't stop stressing about Santana. I didn't like that he would be silent for a while and then show up to harass me. It was no way for me to live, always wondering when next he would appear. I needed peace, and the only way I would have it would be to rid myself of Santana. But how?

I texted Arianna but got no response. I was beginning to worry that she wasn't answering.

Chapter 14

I ended up getting home much later than I wanted to. That was due to fact that although Bria said she and her husband would be back at eleven, they didn't end up getting back until three. When they came through the door, I could only laugh and think about what my mom had said. The good thing about it was that I was too tired to think when my body touched the bed, so there was no staying up to stress about Santana.

My mom's loud voice and her footsteps woke me. "Yes. Can someone please come here now? Yes, please. Alexis! Alexis!" She busted into my room, looking frantic.

I sat up in my bed quickly. "What's wrong?"

"The house has been vandalized!"

My heart sped up. I threw the covers back and jumped from the bed. I ran past my mother, out of my room, and down the stairs. She followed after me. I got downstairs, but everything looked in place. I looked questioningly at my mother.

"Follow me," she said.

I followed her outside and looked around the exterior of the house, horrified. Not only were our cars spray painted with the words *bitch*, *tramp,* and *ho*, but the exterior of the house was also spray painted. Whoever did it was slick enough to bust out the cameras we had around the house.

"You know who the fuck did this shit!"

I closed my eyes briefly. Santana. I mean, it would have to be. Heat rushed to my face. He just wasn't going to stop!

The sounds of sirens blared, and soon a patrol car came pulling into our driveway. The officers got out of their patrol car and surveyed the damage. They both stood with their hands on their hips, taking mental notes.

Before they could get any words out, my mom yelled, "I know who did this!"

"Who?" the officer who'd been driving asked.

"My son. Long story short, I gave him up for adoption when I was sixteen, and he came back into our lives six years ago, and it has been hell ever since. He wants to hurt me and my kids. He is a dangerous man, and if you guys don't catch him, he is going to kill us!"

"Okay." He pulled out a note pad with an arched right brow. "Do you have any proof?"

"I mean, no, but I know it's him, officers."

"Well, it doesn't work like that. I see you have video cameras. Have you viewed the footage?"

She pulled out her phone and logged onto our security system and handed it to one of the officers. He studied it for a couple minutes.

"There is someone on the video, but he is wearing a mask. And there is more than one person. It is not enough to convict this person. We'll have to get forensics over here to sweep the area. What's the name of the person you suspect?"

"Santana Marcelino," I said.

"Do you have an address?"

"No, sir."

As he wrote, he said, "Okay. I will file the report, but that's the most that will come of it right now."

"So that's not enough to arrest him?"

"No. As I already said, we will send someone to come back to fingerprint for evidence. Without more proof, it will be difficult to prove who did the damage."

He took my mother's and my information. When he was done writing, he handed my mother a folded piece of paper. "Here is the report form. If you have any further questions, call the number on this form. Make sure you give them the report number for reference."

With that, they walked away.

"Got damnit! there has got to be something more y'all can do!"

They didn't respond. They simply got in their patrol car and drove out of our driveway.

I ran in the house and went to my room. I threw on some clothes and a pair of shoes as fast as I could, grabbed my phone, keys, and purse. I ran past my mother.

She asked, "Where are you going?"

"I'll be back, Mom."

I had to figure a way out of this. I hopped in my car and raced over to Arianna's house. Once I got there, I breathed a sigh of relief to see her truck still in the driveway.

I jumped out my car ran up the steps and hit her doorbell two times in urgency.

I heard one of her sons say, "Mommy, someone is at the door."

Seconds later, Arianna said, "Who is it?"

"Alexis."

She opened the door quickly. "Hey, girl."

"I really need to talk to you . . . and your husband!"

Chapter 15

Not even five minutes into my conversation, Arianna texted her husband and told him to come home. All it took was for me to say Santana was coming back around.

"He'll be here in about twenty minutes. Alexis, I really wish you had told me sooner."

"I'm sorry. I felt it was my problem, and I didn't want to drag you or your husband into this. But now the situation is so out of control."

"No worries. But just know, for future reference, we're here for you."

"Thanks."

Arianna made us both cups of coffee, and we sipped them while we waited for her husband. I couldn't believe it had come to this, that I was asking my friend and her husband to intervene in my affairs. I thought I was strong enough and smart enough to deal with it on my own. Now I knew Santana was too crazy for me to handle alone. I was thankful to have Arianna in my corner.

Once he arrived, he sat down across from us, and I rehashed everything that Santana had been doing. He sat there and shook his head.

"Sounds like a very sick and deranged individual."

"He is, baby," Arianna said.

"Now, you don't have any type of address on him?"

I shook my head. "No. That's why we weren't able to file the protective order."

"Right. You always have to have a physical address, because if you don't, they have nowhere to serve."

"Right."

"Do you know anything else about him? His family? Friends? Anything?"

"Just a woman he used to mess with that stays in Long Beach. But that was years ago. I don't know if they are still in contact."

"Do you remember the address?"

I racked my brain, but it didn't come to me. "I just know it's on the north side of Long Beach. Other than that, I honestly don't know."

"Because of my job and different breaches, I can't do anything from that end. But I do know an investigator who could get you all the information you need. Has he ever called you or anything?"

"Yes." I took out my phone and showed the number he called me from.

He went to the notes in his iPhone and put the information in. "Give me his name and birthdate if you have it."

I did, and he also texted this into his phone.

"Worst case scenario. I can at least have someone do a mark up and get you his address if the phone is in his name. If I can find anything, I will get the information to you. Let me also have your parole officer's name and number."

I supplied him with that information as well.

"When do you see her again?"

"In two weeks."

"Okay. It's best if you let me talk to her, but I want to have something to present to her when I do. Me being a DA holds a little more leverage than you being her client. The last thing you want is for her to turn on you since he has a romantic involvement with her."

"Thank you for all your help."

"No problem. Be safe."

I hugged them both and left. I spent the rest of the day cleaning up the mess Santana had made. We had ADT come out and fix the cameras and add more. Someone came out and repaired all the windows, and my and my mother's cars were placed at the body shop to get fixed. My mother even went as far as hiring a security guard to sit outside of our house to make things safe. He was a huge guy who said he did security for celebrities as well.

My mom said this was all too much for her, and she went into her room.

I ended up staying up and lying in my bed, only I didn't sleep. My mind raced and raced. So many different scenarios went off in my head—bad ones in reference to what else he might do, and ones that showed a different outcome had I just made a different choice. Regret was a powerful emotion, and at that moment, it had a strong hold on me. Thing was, I knew I just had to stop doing that to myself. I had to stop it, because it would never change where I was now, even if it felt real.

The thing with Dannon . . . He was a really great guy. I had no worries. He never cheated. I never found any-thing on him, and yes, I had looked. That was a man that it seemed like God Himself designed for a woman worthy of him. There was never the slightest bit of flirtation. He said and showed that I was the only women he needed. So, for me to fuck that up . . . it's past just the wrongdoing of it and where it landed him. It was also the fact that there were so many good women out in the world that didn't have the slightest idea of what being truly loved and cherished felt like. Despite being good, they were beat down, cheated on, verbally abused, and often all three. Despite being good women, they never knew what it felt like to have a good man. Some actually went their whole life without knowing one. And there I was with one; after all the other good luck that I had, I had a man like him.

I had taken the opportunity of another woman being blessed with Dannon, and that . . . that was wrong. If I had no longer wanted to be with him, I could have just left him, not let him see me having sex with another man when he was supposed to be my world. That alone was horrible.

It was funny that a lot of women I was locked up with said they would have given up all they had to know what the love Dannon gave me felt like. I found it so interesting and so very sad that it took for me to be locked up to understand that, because I always had it. I never knew the other side.

My phone started ringing. I looked at the caller. It was James.

I answered it quickly. "Hello?"

"Hey. What you got going on?"

"Some stuff you wouldn't believe or want to believe."

"Why don't you try me?"

"No, I don't want to talk about it. It will just get me down again."

"Well, shit. Okay. You want some company?"

"I live with my mom, James."

"Well, come to me so we can be two miserable moth-afuckas together."

I chuckled. "I don't have my car."

"Get dressed and text me your address. See you in a bit."

Damn. Is he asking me or telling me? He wasn't kidding when he said he was an alpha male. I didn't really like that he was being so alpha, but I needed the company. It would get my mind off what I was dealing with. I jumped up and threw on a sweat suit and a pair of flip-flops, brushed a comb through my hair, and brushed my teeth.

When James texted me and said he was outside, I went to check on my mom. She was asleep. There was a bottle of Ambien on the bedside table. She had admitted to me that ever since I had started dating Santana, she had problems sleeping. I assumed her solution was to take medication. I think prison just intensified her restlessness.

I didn't feel like being out and about, so James picked up some food from The Cheesecake Factory, and we went back to his place. It was a nice three-bedroom home. I was impressed by his choice in design and furniture. I was expecting a sparse bachelor pad, but it felt cozy and comfortable.

"This is nice," I said.

"What did you expect?"

"I don't know. Not this."

"Oh, you thought I was some cheap nigga with no taste."

"I didn't say that. You said that."

"Well, I take pride in my home. I like nice things."

"It shows."

He laid out all the food on the coffee table. We had nachos, salmon rolls, and popcorn shrimp.

"Where are your sons?" I asked.

"With their aunt, which is my late wife's sister. She is taking them to Sea World this weekend."

We sat in his living room on the couch. I tried to force some food down, but I ate very little because I was still unsettled by the events with Santana.

"So, what was going on with you?"

"Typical BS." I didn't want to get into detail about Santana and all of his antics. There was no need for James to know about any of it. I just had to have faith that Arianna's husband would be able to help me and my mother.

"Anything you want to talk about?"

I shook my head, but even as I did, tears instantly started flowing down my cheeks. The pressure was getting to me.

James scooted closer to me and wrapped one of his arms around me. "Hey, hey, hey." He wiped the tears off my face with one of his fingers. "I do not like seeing a woman cry. I used to be unmoved by it. I was like this person who was detached from other people's emotions. That damn Allure. She taught me all about empathy. After her, I could never sit and let another woman be down, whether her crying has something to do with me or not. So, just know you can speak to me. I'm here."

"Thanks, James."

"No problem." His eyes locked with mine. Then, out of nowhere, he leaned over and kissed me.

I froze for a moment, and so did he. As he pulled away, I placed my hand on his crotch. He looked down at my hand, then back at my face. I could feel him harden against my hand. He took my hand off and stood to his feet.

I stood too. Before he could say anything, I said, "I'm sorry. I didn't mean to disrespect you. It's just that—"

"What?"

"With me being locked up, it's been five yea—"

Before I could finish, James hungrily kissed me. I kissed him back with the same passion. He picked me up like I was a baby and carried me to his bedroom. We kissed the entire way. He tossed me on his bed; then he lunged over me and grabbed the buttons on my jeans.

He pulled them off, all while saying, "Five years? We gotta do something about that." Then he tossed my legs apart and went to town on my pussy. He licked the folds of my flesh before heading his mouth over to my clit, which he sucked gently all while fingering me.

Man, I felt like I was dying. His mouth on me reminded me of getting my pussy licked for the first time. I pushed my head back into the pillow and screamed at the top of my lungs. Then, as he continued to lick me, he massaged my asshole. My legs started to shake, and I felt so weak I couldn't hold them up in the air. He wrapped one around the back of his neck and held one in the air with his free hand. Then his mouth went to my asshole, and he started sucking there, all while his fingers kept fingering my pussy. It was all I could take before I squirted all in his face. He laughed, raised his head, and wiped it off with his shirt. Then he took the palm of my hand and slapped the face of my pussy with it.

He stood, stripped out of his clothes, and went to one of his drawers. I admired his firm, naked, muscular physique. When I was locked up, it was something I never thought I would actually see again—a naked man. He turned back around and faced me. He had a condom hanging off of his erect dick. It was so fat and long. I shivered in anticipation of how it would feel inside of me.

He walked back over to the bed and climbed on top of me and grasped my thighs between his hands. I was already creamy when he mounted me, and when I felt his dick enter me, my eyelids fluttered, and I moaned low in my throat. He barely got two strokes in before I started nutting and convulsing. Still, he continued to stroke in and out of me. First, he went slow; then he sped it up. He stared down at me and laughed.

He leaned down and suckled on both of my nipples all while raking my insides. When I say I was wet, it is an understatement. Fluid continued to leak out of me, and every time he entered and exited, you could hear gurgling sounds. James threw his head back and laughed super loud, but I was too into the array of sensations he was making my body feel: hot all over my body, my feet continued to get the chills. And he kept on going, stroking in and out swiftly, keeping the momentum going. When he stuck a finger in my asshole, I exploded, and so much cum seeped out of me that it soaked my bottom and the sheets! And what's more, I couldn't stop screaming and moaning. I was feeling the orgasm well after James was done.

He just lay on his forearms and continued to laugh at me, saying, "Damn, I have never seen any shit like that before."

James had sex with me three more times that day. I was out of it, and with the blackout curtains, I didn't realize that it was morning until he came in the room with a cup of coffee for me. I sipped it, and the night before replayed in my head. That man had fucked the shit out of me. And despite doing it four times, I wanted more. In fact, my pussy was pulsating at the thought of more of his loving.

The ride back to my house with James was pretty quiet. Honestly, I don't think either of us knew quite what to say. I mean, we barely knew each other, yet we had shared something so intimate over and over. I chuckled just thinking about it.

"What?" he asked.

"Nothing." I shook my head with a big Kool-Aid smile on my face.

"Ummm, you lying. And you're not a good liar, either. Something on your mind?"

"Can you just let me be?" I asked with a smile on my face.

My phone vibrated, telling me I had a missed call.

As he drove down the street, a car suddenly cut him off by jumping in front of him without signaling. James had to hit his brakes quickly. He simply shook his head and continued.

"Well, there is something on my mind," he said.

"What would that be, James?"

"You know I've never been with a woman—"

Suddenly, the car in front of us swerved over to the right, causing James to hit his brakes again.

"What is wrong with this fool?"

I looked to my right as the crazy driver rolled down his window. I gasped. It was Santana. He raised a gun from his lap and pointed it in our direction.

"James!"

James looked at me, then out the window at Santana. Santana started firing his gun at us. James and I both ducked down, and James increased the speed. Santana chased after us and continued to fire his gun. James swerved into the other lane, nearly colliding with another car, but that didn't stop Santana from racing after us.

"Who the fuck is this fool?" James accelerated his speed.

I reached for my phone and called 911.

"Nine one one. What is your emergency?"

"There is a driver shooting at us! We are driving down South Street in Long Beach. Please hurry."

I scanned the streets, praying for a cop car.

James turned down another street, and it looked like we had lost Santana. But we were wrong. He had crept to James's left, and he fired more shots. That's when I saw James's body jerk. Blood splattered all over the place. I screamed at the top of my lungs, anticipating one of the bullets claiming my life.

James lost control of the car as he fought for his life. The car swerved off the road and slammed into a street light. The airbag deployed and stopped me from smashing my skull against the dashboard. The impact knocked me out and cracked a rib.

Chapter 16

I took a deep breath as I sat in the hospital, trying to calmly answer the questions officers had, all while James was in ICU. James had been shot in his left shoulder and had lost a lot of blood. The bullet lodged close to his heart, so the surgery to remove it was extremely delicate. The surgeons successfully removed the bullet, but it would be a day or two until they could fully assess the damage.

"So, do you know this person?" the officer asked me.

"Yes, sir. His name is Santana Marcelino."

"How do you know him personally? Is he an ex-boy-friend or related to you?"

"Yes."

"Yes to which one? *Which is he*?"

I closed my eyes briefly. "He is my half-brother."

"Why would your brother want to kill you?"

"Listen, the man is crazy. He is trying to harm my entire family. He vandalized my home just the other day. My mother, my sister, and I are all unsafe with him around."

"What does he look like? And I need details on the vehicle. The make, model, color, and year if you know."

I gave him as vivid a description of Santana as I could. I only remembered the car was a black Honda. I didn't know the other details.

"Anything else you want to add?"

I shook my head.

He gave me his card and a piece of paper. "That's a protective order. This one is an emergency order, and you have to go to court to get a permanent order issued. I'll have the judge sign off on it today. If he comes near you or your property, call the police."

"Thank you."

The officer rose to his feet and left.

I stayed at the hospital until James was released from surgery, but I was not allowed to see him. Nonetheless, I stayed at the hospital. My mom called me nonstop, demanding to know where I was. I simply texted her and told her I had stayed over a guy friend's house and not to worry.

The next morning, I woke up in the ICU waiting room. My neck was sore from the awkward position I had slept in the chair. It took me a second to remember where I was and what had happened. Once I was oriented, I hounded the nurses to let me see James, since he was now listed in stable condition.

When I went into the room, all I could do was pull my lips in to keep from crying. True, he was okay, but still, seeing him hooked up to all those machines and all the noise they were generating reminded me that he and I both could have lost our lives the day before. And I wasn't concerned about mine. I was concerned about his, because just his affiliation with me could have left him in a body bag and his boys fatherless. That hurt like hell to know, and it just wasn't right.

His movements were slow when we made eye contact as I came to stand by his bed. I offered a smile as best I could, even though I knew it was tight.

"Hey."

He cleared his throat and said, "Hey."

"How are you feeling?"

"Like shit. But I'm alive, so I'm not complaining at all."

I chuckled.

"Did you know that mothafucka?"

I slowly nodded my head.

"Who was he, and why in the fuck did he try to kill us?"

"Listen. My half-brother. The one I told you I was sleeping with at one point."

"That's him?"

I nodded. "I'm so sorry to get you involved in this."

"Alexis, I don't blame you at all. He is a fool. And you shouldn't blame yourself either. I hope you aren't."

Tears slid down my face. Man, I wish it were that easy, for someone to say those magic words and for the hurt to go away. But it just wasn't. By the grace of God, James had survived the ambush, but what if he hadn't? It would have been more blood on my hands based on bad decisions I made five years before.

I started sobbing uncontrollably.

"Don't do that. Come here."

But I shook my head instead and backed away from him. "I can't see you anymore."

"Why?"

"You have two boys who need you. You don't get just how demented this man is. He is hell bent on destroying me, and he does not care who else goes down in the process. So, I have to stay away from you, and—" I swallowed, thinking of how sweet he was to me the day before. Who knows where this could have gone? Maybe more sex, and only sex, or maybe more dates, maybe a commitment, meeting each other's families, marriage, maybe kids. That might have been a possibility in another time and in another place. I wanted it. I had always wanted to settle down. I had that chance before, and I blew it. Now those past mistakes were haunting again. My voice cracked when I said, "I just have to stay away from you."

"Alexis."

"And you. You have to stay away from me."

"Alexis, I don't want to stay away. I like you, and you like me. We can deal with that crazy—"

I shook my head, leaned over, and kissed him on his lips. Then, before he could grab me with the little strength he had, I pulled away and backed away from him.

"Alexis, don't do that. Wait!"

But I was only a few steps from the door. I ran those last steps, and before he could stop me, I exited the hospital room. I ran to the bathroom down the hall, locked myself in a stall, and cried. I was going to be paying the price for my selfishness for the rest of my life. I was destined to never have peace.

Chapter 17

I took an Uber to the house and continued to cry all the way there. It was becoming clear the only way to have peace would be if one of us killed the other. Sad thing to say, but both of us living in this world just wouldn't work. Sad that I had really thought if I righted all the wrongs I had done, I could have a life again and be happy. Now I saw that just wasn't in the cards for me. It seemed I was going to have to take extreme measures in order to live a normal life.

I took my phone out of my purse and saw my parole agent had called me. It was weird because she called late, like two in the morning. I had a funny feeling looking at that missed call. It was also strange that she didn't leave a message. I was sure it had to do with Santana. There was no way I wanted to get on her bad side, so I started to call her back when another call came through.

"Hello?"

"Alexis Vancamp?"

Yes."

"This is Detective Green. I believe we have the suspect in custody. Would you feel comfortable coming down and positively identifying him?"

Praise God! I thought. They had Santana, and that was fast! Maybe there still was hope for me. If I could get this man locked up, then my family and I would be free!

"Yes. Give me a minute. I'm gonna change clothes, and I will be there as soon as I can."

I raced to my room and jumped in the shower. I used a bar of soap and scrubbed my body to get all the blood from James off me. Obviously, I didn't know him for that long, yet it still had hurt, the thought of having to completely cut him out my life. The pain was like I said: who knows where it could have led? But now, with Santana finally being in custody, maybe that would reopen the opportunity to see where we could go.

I rinsed the soap off of me, grabbed a towel, wrapped it around myself, and went into my bedroom. I quickly dried off, grabbed underwear and a bra out of my drawer, and pulled them on quickly. Then I threw on a pair of jeans and a T-shirt. Before I could get a pair of socks and sneakers on, I heard the doorbell. I knew it couldn't be Santana, so the threat was not there. There was no one else who wanted to hurt me.

I raced down the stairs and disengaged the alarm. When I opened the door, I was surprised to see my parole agent.

"I have been calling you nonstop since yesterday."

"Sorry. I only saw you had called late last night. I was meaning to call you back, but some stuff hap—"

She looked around and asked, "Is anyone home?"

"No."

"Could I come inside?"

I narrowed my eyes at her. She looked really shaken up, and normally, when she came for field visits, she never asked permission. She just barged her way in.

"Yes." Her visits were always quick. Five minutes wouldn't hurt me from going down to the police station. I stepped aside and let her in.

Once she entered the house, she simply stood there wringing her hands. For the first time, I saw how fearful she was. It was unlike her to be so nervous. She had always been a person to show her dominance and assert her power, especially over me, her parolee.

"Alexis, I need to talk to you, and it's not about your parole." Her eyes got watery, and her hands started shaking. "Before you say anything that is going to bruise my soul, just listen to me. I been fucking him. I think I love him! But something is off about him. Nothing makes sense. Where he says he comes from, who his parents are, what he does for a living. . . . So, the parole agent in me that investigates investigated. And guess what? It led me to you. I put a GPS on his car, and he keeps driving by your house.

"I know I'm in a position to lose my job, and this is so stupid to do this over a man. Truth be told, I don't even know how I ended up in this damn situation. Not long after you got released, I met him, and my life ain't been the same ever since. Although I don't know much about him because everything is a damn mystery, I can't get this man out of my system. But I have to know your connection to him. Are you fucking him?"

"No, I'm not."

She exhaled, but then she paused. "Well, have you ever slept with him?"

I looked down. "Yes. Over five years ago."

Relief flooded her face at the notion that I slept with him before she knew him.

"Listen to me very carefully. Santana is a very dangerous man. You need to stay away from him. He really means you no good."

Her blank expression showed me she wasn't shook by any of this. I think her main concern was whether he was sleeping with me.

"How do you know this? How do you know *him*?" she said passively.

I took a deep breath. "You may want to sit down for this."

I proceeded to tell her about my history with Santana, making sure to give her all the information. Not one detail was left out. Twenty minutes later, she sat back from me, stunned. Her lips moved, but no sound came out. I'd obviously made an impression on her. She was truly trying to grasp and comprehend what I'd just released on her.

Then she burst out crying. "Oh God, what have I got myself into?"

"I felt the same way. But the good part is you can heed my warning and stay away from that man forever."

"I wish I could. Girl, I'm pregnant by him."

I gasped. *Damn!* "What are you going to do?"

"My family knows. There is no way I can abort this baby. So, I'm going to be tied to a psychopath for the rest of my life. And sad part is I love him. What the fuck is wrong with me? Nothing you said has shifted the way I feel about him." She sobbed miserably.

"I've been there. Believe me, I have. But I'm telling you first-hand what you are dealing with. He is a monster. It is imperative stay away from him. He will ruin your life. He's still coming after me. It freaks me out that he drives by my home as much as you say. There is no end to his psychosis. The reason I didn't call you back was because I was at the hospital. Yesterday, Santana followed me and shot me and my friend while we were driving. He tried to kill me."

"Yesterday? He told me he had to go out of town. Damn, I can't believe he is doing all this stuff to you. So, he's locked up?"

I nodded. "Yes. They caught him."

"Well, maybe that is what I need to push me to stay the hell away from him." She stood to her feet. "This thing with me and him was never real. He played me. How could I be so stupid, yet I'm still yearning for him?" She shook her head and wiped her face free of tears. "I should know better. With this job, I run into con artists all the time, and I never once thought he was one. I have given this man money, paid his bills, even had a threesome with him. I'm sure you think I'm an idiot."

"You'll get no judgment from me. I've been in the exact same position as you." And I meant it. It wasn't hard falling for Santana. He was a good lover and convincing with his words.

"Thanks. I misjudged you."

I offered a smile.

As she reached for the door knob, she looked back at me and said, "Listen, I know I'm asking for a lot, but can this conversation stay between the both of us?"

"Yes. I won't mention it."

"You know, I really thought I had found my Prince Charming."

Deep down, I knew that if it weren't for the fact that Santana would probably get a lot of time for attempting to kill me and James, she would still deal with him despite the risk he posed to her life. I actually wasn't sure she wouldn't still stick by him even after everything I had told her. But I got it; I'd been there. Her stakes with her job seem a little higher, but I think she was just operating off her emotions and not common sense.

Why couldn't it have been that clear to me when I was in it? I guess I had to go through it to understand the fucked-up choices I was making for that man. Well, if I could help one other woman avoid the mistakes I made, then I felt like it would all be worth it in the end.

When she opened the door, I gasped as Santana appeared. She tried to shove the door closed, but he easily stopped it. I screamed as he kicked the door, hitting her directly in her face, causing blood to stream down her face.

Then he barged right in and said, "You stupid, nosy-ass bitch." He slapped her across her face.

I wanted to help her, but I was afraid he would unleash on me so I stood there, frozen, as he grabbed her by her hair and slammed her head into the coffee table repeatedly. I gasped as her body froze then went limp. When he released her, I took off running. He chased after me and dragged me back by my hair over to where my parole agent lay. Blood continued seeping from the gash on her forehead and streamed from her nose. She looked dead. I closed my eyes and sobbed. He tossed blood in my face and forced my hands around her neck. He then pulled out his cell phone.

I screamed, and he punched me in my mouth. I cried out in pain as the brutal force of his fist caused the inside of my mouth to mash against my teeth.

"Make another sound and I'll break your face, bitch."

I cringed at the sight of his fist in my face. He dialed 911.

"Tell them your name and that you just killed some-one, or I'll bash you in the fucking head!"

Chapter 18

Two and a half months later.

And there I was, sitting in jail, staring at the iron bars of my cell. It felt like a dream. I had tasted sweet freedom for a short time, and there I was back in hell. It was the same sterile institutional smell, the constant noise of inmates and guards, the never-ending harassment from guards on power trips. I closed my eyes, wishing it away. It was a nightmare that I couldn't wake up from.

After Santana had given me the phone and I told the police what he told me to say, he ran out of my house. When I called back and tried to explain, they told me to let the officers they dispatched know. But they weren't having it. I should have run, but I was afraid that Santana would be waiting, and I stupidly trusted that the police would believe me.

The police surrounded the house with guns drawn and came like raging bulls in the house. They took one look at Ms. Wilkes, yanked me by my hair, and placed me in handcuffs.

"Listen, I didn't do it. It was Santana! Please listen to me," I pleaded.

"Shut the fuck up. You already confessed. You're done!"

After they cuffed me, they threw me in the back of the police car so fast and rough I thought they had dislocated my shoulder.

You're done! You're done! You're done! Those words continued to ring in my head. He was right; there was no way I was going to get out of this. I tried to put on a brave face and stay positive, but I was terrified. The tease of freedom made my time in jail even worse this time.

Because it was on the news and considered a high-profile case, I was in front of a judge within forty-eight hours. I pleaded not guilty to the charge of attempted murder—attempted only because Ms. Wilkes's heart was still beating, but due to the head trauma, she was unconscious in intensive care. According to the DA, the doctors said she more than likely wouldn't pull through. So, my only witness couldn't even open her eyes. My only shot of beating the case was on the edge of death, which would change my charge to murder.

My lawyer tried to get me bail, but I was denied because I'd already been convicted of murder once before. I was forced to sit in Twin Towers until my next hearing. I felt cold inside when they denied bail and used my prior conviction as a reason. I knew it wasn't looking good for me.

The only positive that came from lockup was that they placed me in the kitchen, but that caused tension with the other five inmates who worked in there. They'd been working together for a while and didn't trust outsiders. What made it even worse was that the head cook was their friend, and the guard that decided to place me there had fired her.

The day the guard informed me I would take the position, she said, "Listen I want to shake things up in there. Let them know they are not running the kitchen or dictating what goes on around here. So, get the kitchen in order and don't get punked. I would have went down the list, but the next five in line either have a smart-ass mouth or is affiliated with them."

To that, I simply nodded.

The girls I worked with didn't say much to me, as me being the head cook, I could get rid of them. I did the job the way they asked me to and kept my mouth shut, but that didn't stop the constant tension with the workers and that particular guard. Every day of her shift, her post was the kitchen. When I worked, I would look up every couple seconds, and the same guard was watching all of them like a hawk. Every now and then, one would toss a look her way, but she would always catch it and stare them down, almost sneering, and they would look away.

To be honest, Ms. Carter brought the hostility on herself. She had a way of talking to them that was very condescending, demeaning, and disrespectful. She would tell them they wasn't worth shit. Once, she told one of them, a girl named Willis, "You know, the world would be a better place if your mom had been swallowed . . . nut in the jaw." Then she tossed her head back and laughed.

When the girl looked at her hatefully, she said, "The fuck you gonna do? I got the gun."

But the thing was, the jails were an interesting place, because morals and values were interchangeable among inmates and guards. You could be a guard and a bad person, or you could be an inmate and a good person. That always made things more dangerous, because you never knew who you could trust. Who was truly the good guy? So, I kept to my damn self. While us women certainly didn't have the strength the men had, there were definitely women getting attacked, jumped, and even slashed there. It was no place I needed to be.

With only a month until my trial, I was beginning to lose hope. I hated that shit. Prison seemed like my future. My biggest fear was never getting out. I mean, I had been given a second chance the first time. I wasn't trying to be negative, but what were the chances to be found not guilty of a crime you're not guilty of when it looks like you're guilty?

I thought back to my first visit during the first week I was there.

It was a Saturday. When I walked out, I saw my mother and sister were seated at the booth. I smiled and sat down across from them.

My mother took the phone first. She smiled at me in a loving motherly way.

"Ugh. How are you?"

To not worry her, I said, "Good. Good, Mom."

She eyed me up and down. "You are already losing weight."

"Well, I'm working in the kitchen. Keeps me busy and the pounds off."

She took a deep breath. "I hope that's what it is. The lawyer tried his damndest to get the bail. But don't worry. We are going to get you out of here, baby."

I smiled. "I know, Mom."

"And listen, I just want to let you know that I am so proud of you. When you got out, you made amends with everyone. The old Alexis washed away. I mean, it's like the Bible said: renewed in the mind. You showed so much humility and repaired all strained relationships. I can't say it enough how much incredible growth you have shown, baby. Alexis, you have your life ahead of you, and so many beautiful moments that you deserve are ahead of you. Just keep praying and hoping and stay strong."

My mom's words made me feel so much better, almost as if no matter what happened to me, if I never got out, I had managed to meet my goal when I got out of prison, and that was to make it right with everyone I had wronged.

My sister then pushed my mother out of the way and grabbed the phone.

"Sister!" She had tears in her eyes.

"Hey, Bria."

"This is such bullsh—. It's not right. But don't worry; we got your back. The church is behind you one hundred percent. We have a fund going for you to help with the lawyer fees, and the church told me to tell you that they are all praying for you. That sick bastard is not going to get away with this shit."

"Stop cursing, First Lady."

"Sorry." She chuckled despite the situation.

"Bria, I love you," I told her.

"I love you too, big sister. I need you."

"You got me, Bria. Always. Even when I'm not around, I'm always praying for you." And I meant that, because I was. Once I got my mind right after my incarceration, I started it. I prayed for her, my father, and my mother. I prayed for all three of them more than I even prayed for myself.

My mother's eyes got watery at that moment. She looked away quickly and coughed, clearing her throat. After a pregnant pause, my mother took the phone back.

"Now, you know they still haven't found that bastard."

"Still?"

"Still."

I looked away. That meant my family was still in danger, and I couldn't do anything for anyone being locked up. I didn't understand why the detective had called me that day and said they had caught him. They must have had the wrong person, because that surely was Santana's crazy ass on my doorstep the day my parole agent came.

"Don't worry. They will find him. That's a fact. Arianna sends her love, by the way. She said her husband can't get involved because of conflict of interest, and since this made the news, she can't come to see you. But what they did find out is that he has no criminal history out here. But he has a rap sheet in Perris, California. That's why it's so hard to find him."

I nodded. I understood. Arianna's husband was an LA County district attorney. It wouldn't be a good idea for them to get involved. But it sure would help having them on board, because her husband knew about the law. Still, I would just have to hope my lawyer stayed on top of this.

"It's crazy. This man shot at me and another person in broad daylight, and they can't find him?"

"If they ever do. But listen, don't think negatively. There is some hope."

Before my mother could finish, the alarms blared and guards came out, shouting, "All inmates on your feet! We are on lock-down!"

I couldn't even say another word to my mom or hear what the hope was before guards were shoving us in a line and ordering us back to our tier and cell.

"What's going on?" I asked the girl behind me.

"Bitches are acting out. There was a riot on the yard, so they shutting stuff down."

I shook my head. I blew kisses to my sister and my mom before turning around in the line.

But as time winded down, one week turned to two, then a month turned into another month. I honestly had doubt I would get out. Just as I was losing all hope and actually considering ending my life, my lawyer came to visit. I proceeded to our meeting with not much hope.

He got right to the point of his visit. "Ms. Wilkes is awake, and she gave us a statement vindicating you."

I gasped. Relief flooded me. "What does that mean? Am I getting out of here?"

"I'm not waiting for the trial date. I'm going to contact the judge's clerk and see if we can advance and vacate the court date and have this heard sooner, so you can get out of here and catch the real killer."

"Thank you so much!"

I went back to my cell, stunned. I tried to stay calm, but I couldn't sit still. I was anxious and excited. I kept pacing and dancing to the joyous music in my head. I was going to be free.

"Vancamp? Are we doing oranges or fruit cocktail?" one of the workers asked me, taking me out of my thoughts. She was standing near the small office I was sitting in.

"You can do oranges," I said. Then I turned my attention back to the inventory sheets I was going over. From the glass windows, I could see the other four workers in the kitchen. One was slicing the roast beef for din-

ner, another was placing the rolls on the tray for the serving line, while the other was prepping for our breakfast
the next morning. The guard was tucked away in a corner
on her cell phone. The only thing on my mind was getting the hell out of there. Ms. Wilkes had made a recovery, and thank God, she was willing to give a written
statement my lawyer could use to get me out of jail. Who
would have thought she would survive the head injury?
Now the question was, would she go down for her
involvement with Santana? I hoped not. But who knew
how it was going to play out? One thing for sure, it was a
lesson learned for her.

I wondered if she had lost the baby. And truthfully,
now that she knew what a despicable person Santana
was, if she hadn't lost it, did she still want it? Babies
are beautiful and a gift, but the baby would be a constant
reminder of Santana. I know it would be difficult for me
if I had to make that choice.

The sounds of alarms took me out of my thoughts and
made me instantly panic. Now what was going on?

We all froze and heard, "This facility is now on lock-
down."

Damn, again?

Ms. Carter panicked and started yelling for us to
all take a knee. She then went to the phone and started
dialing. That's when all the inmates in the kitchen
rushed her from behind. I gasped, as they were able to
unarm her. She screamed for her life as they attacked
her. The inmates repeatedly stomped her in the head.
The only one that didn't do anything was Willis. She
stood by while the others continued to attack her.

I ran out of the office and proceeded to shove them
away from her, yelling, "Stop before you kill her!" But

all that did was anger them, because one grabbed me by my hair, while another swung on me, cracking me in my left jaw and knocking me backward, causing me to lose my balance.

"Stay the fuck out of it!" one of them yelled.

I sat there dazed for a moment. I stayed on the floor and watched them continue to assault Ms. Carter. It looked like she was out cold, but their hatred of her wouldn't let them leave well enough alone. I couldn't sit back and watch someone get beat to death, no matter how nasty the person was, so I threw myself on top of her and took the hits and the kicks. And while they were painful, they were bearable to stop them from causing any more hurt to Ms. Carter. But suddenly, I felt a pain unlike like any of the hits or kicks. Because it wasn't.

I felt a cold blade jab into my back viciously. I froze for a second, paralyzed by my pain. I screamed when I was stabbed again. When the blade was removed, I managed to flip over onto my back to see Willis hovering over me and Ms. Carter. She drove the knife down into my stomach then stabbed Ms. Carter. She stabbed wherever she could hit. The repeated stabbing was sapping my strength. I struggled to fight back. I put up my hand to try to block the attack. Willis pushed it aside and continued her attack. My mouth opened to plead with her, but no sound came out. She saw this and smiled; then her faced morphed into a hateful glare. The other women backed up. My eyes pleaded with them to help, but they wouldn't. They ran from the kitchen instead. As blood oozed out of me, so did my breath, until I felt myself slipping away.

Chapter 19

The attack from Willis caused lateral stab wounds and kept me in the medical mod for a month. The doctor said I was lucky my chest cavity didn't fill up with blood or that Willis didn't hit a major artery, or I would have lost my life that day. It turns out Willis had found out the night before that her mother had passed. I guess the comment Ms. Carter had told her, "The world would be better if your mom had been swallowed." She just couldn't let it ride. Guess she was at a point where she didn't care about anything anymore but getting Ms. Carter. I just happened to be collateral damage, or better yet, a casualty of war. The good part was that Ms. Carter and I both survived.

While recovering, I found out that the judge had granted my trial date be moved up. I pleaded with the doctor to let me go, but he wouldn't release me. I was disappointed that I couldn't be there. I wanted to witness the judge saying, "Case dismissed."

The morning of the trial, I woke up early. I pleaded with the doctor one last time to release me to the trial. He wasn't changing his mind. The rest of the day, I was restless. The nurses kept coming in to check on me because my heart rate was higher than normal. I was anxious to hear the outcome of the trial. It wasn't guaranteed that the motion would be dismissed. What if Ms. Wilkes changed her testimony? There was a part of me that feared Santana had gotten to her and convinced her to change her story. I felt helpless lying in that bed, unable to personally tell my story. It was all in the hands of my lawyer and Ms. Wilkes.

Late in the afternoon, my lawyer came to see me. I tried to read his expression as he walked in, but his face was neutral. I didn't have a good feeling. He sat down and looked at me with sympathetic eyes. My heart sank.

"How are you feeling?" he asked.

"Fine. What happened today?"

"I'm sorry you weren't able to be there."

"Just tell me."

"I wish you could have seen it. Ms. Wilkes testified that Santana was the one that attacked her, and the judge threw the case out instantly. She then issued a warrant for the arrest of Santana."

I sat up in bed. "Are you serious?"

"It was beautiful. The only thing is you can't leave yet. I tried to get you released immediately, but because of bureaucracy, there is paperwork that needs to be filed first. You won't be out of here for a few days. I'll push for it to happen sooner, but there's no guarantee."

"I don't care, as long as I know I'm out of here."

"When you get out, we should talk about suing the State for your attack. They were negligent and responsible. I think we have a great case."

"One thing at a time. Get me out first."

The next few days, I was relaxed and in a great mood. Once word got out that I was innocent and would be getting out, the attitudes of the nurses and doctors changed. They were much more patient and caring. I gave a thought to telling them they were full of shit, but I was feeling good and didn't want to waste my time on their trifling asses.

There was no better feeling than seeing my mother at the pre-release center. I walked in, and she was there waiting for me. I smiled so big my cheeks hurt. She took one look at all the bandages on me and collapsed. Guards rushed to her, and the paramedics were called. The paramedics waved smelling salts under her nose, and her eyes immediately shot open. They checked her out and said she was fine to be released. I signed paperwork, and my mom and I left arm in arm, two women a little worse for wear, but still plugging along.

I closed my eyes as I sat in my mother's car and she drove away from the jail. I couldn't believe my luck. I mean, I survived a stabbing and prison again! I had spent three months locked up for manslaughter and then was almost murdered, and now I was en route to my home. I had no idea how I'd gotten through it all.

As I sat in wonder at my luck, another part of me was worried about what was to come for me. The fact of the matter was that the cops had still not caught Santana. It was only a matter of time before he came out of hiding to make my life hell.

My mother placed one of her hands over mine and squeezed it. I smiled, raised her hand in mine, and kissed it. Then I dozed off in the car.

"Wake me up when we're home, Mom."

"I sure will."

When we made it to the house, my mom tapped me on my shoulder, waking me out of my sleep. I'd been dreaming of being on a beach, sipping on a margarita, feeling the sand between my toes while I watched the waves crash into the beach.

We walked to the steps. All I wanted to do was take a shower, wash the prison off of me, get a good meal, and go back to sleep. However, after my mom opened the living room door, the lights came on suddenly, and I heard several people yell, "Surprise!"

A hand yanked me into the house. I laughed as my sister pulled me in her arms and hugged me in a bear hug. Once she released me, I was hugged by her husband, then Arianna and her husband, and a slew of people from the church. The entire living room was packed with people. It was crazy because it was so different than my other homecoming. At that home coming, there were only a few there, and Bria didn't even want to be there. And now in this moment, Bria couldn't be happier to see me. Dannon's mother was even in attendance and gave me the warmest hug. In fact, I was getting hugs and kisses from everyone. Seeing the house full of people that were there for me was insane. Even Maricela was there with her kids.

There was a DJ, none other than my friend Justin, spinning music. He yelled over the beat, "Welcome home, Alexis."

I smiled at him and blew him a kiss.

"Come dance with me!" Bria said.

"Let her eat first," my mom said, coming forward with a huge plate filled with all kinds of foods similar to the things I ate when I first got out.

Arianna stood close to me, and her husband said, "Let's go outside and talk."

I nodded, and my mother and I followed after them.

"Alexis, I just wanted to give you a heads up. Due to conflict of interest, I can have no dealings with the case, but I wanted to let you know what I know. At the last hearing, a Ramey warrant for Santana was issued by the court."

"What's that?" my mother asked

"A bench warrant. So, it really is just a matter of time before he is detained and charged with the attempted murder of Ms. Wilkes."

"I sure hope so."

"Oh, he will be. So, for now, don't even worry yourself. Justice will be served here." Jabari then kissed his wife and said, "Gotta go get some rest. I have a lot to do tomorrow."

He hugged my mother and me, and we went back into the house.

My mom took one look at my worried face and said, "Don't look like that. Trust me, they are going to get him."

"Yes. I give it twenty-four hours. I mean, he tried to kill a peace officer." Arianna rubbed my back reassuringly. "Smile, girl, and eat some of that food."

I laughed and let their words console me and did as they suggested, eating a juicy and buttery and spicy lobster tail. I looked at the party and saw my sister getting it in on the dance floor. She was bent over, with her hands on her knees, twerking. Ladies from the church looked on disapprovingly. Many were pointing at her and shaking their heads while a few chuckled.

As the music changed to a cut by Drake, my sister started to dance a little wilder and started grinding. My mom shook her head and muttered, "Damn shame."

"Gotta save my li'l sis." I told Arianna and handed her my plate. I then went and joined my sister on the dance floor. Thank God the song changed to the Whip, and I asked her, "Show me how to do this dance." She grabbed one of my hands and taught me step by step. Arianna and her two sons joined us and a few others. I went through the routine as my sister instructed.

My sister laughed and kept saying, "That's it, Alexis!"

People were even cheering for me. The ladies that were looking on disapprovingly were now clapping for us. Casey was even able to pull my mother onto the dance floor.

The love I was receiving, man, felt dynamic. We were all having a good time, like a family. I mean, more than I had ever experienced, even before Santana. The only thing that was missing was my father.

Chapter 20

My sister grabbed me and continued to dance with me, and it seemed like my problems in that moment were nonexistent as we danced to "Freedom" by Beyoncé. I got so into the song that I closed my eyes because, to a huge degree, I felt free. And the things I had wished I had the chance to say, all the things I wished I had the chance to do, I now had. No better feeling was there than to have the love and forgiveness of the people I loved. Yes, Santana was still out there lurking and probably still plotting, but I had to believe Jabari that they would get him, and he would be out of our lives for good.

My sister and I danced until our feet hurt. She was so exhausted that she was lying on the couch with a face towel folded over her head while her husband rubbed her feet. The baby was resting against my chest, knocked out asleep.

"Baby, let's go. I have to get up in the morning," Casey said.

"You too tired to make baby number two?" Bria asked.

Lust filled his face instantly. "I'm never too tired for that, baby."

"I don't want to hear this," my mom said, wiping off the coffee table.

"Anybody wanna babysit so me and hubby can have some alone time?" she asked.

"No! Watch your own baby, because you never seem to know how to pick her up on time!" my mother snapped.

I chuckled. "I'll babysit."

Bria jumped up and kissed me on the cheek. "I swear I love this woman!"

"Not so fast! Do you have diapers and formula for the baby?" my mom demanded.

"Bottle, diapers, wipes, and jammies are in her bag, and there is a canister of Similac in your cabinet, dear mother," Bria said sweetly.

"It better be, Bria, because neither Alexis nor I are going to be getting up in the middle of the night for formula or diapers."

"Relax, Mom." My sister did a hand gesture like she was cracking a whip. "Let's go, honey. Time to get our *Fifty Shades of Grey* on!

I chuckled as my mom shook her head.

"Toodles!" She grabbed her purse and shoes, and in a flash, she and her husband were out the door.

My mother sat down next to me. "The bassinet is in my room. I'll get it whenever you're ready."

"Okay."

"Did you enjoy the party?"

"Yes. Thanks for throwing it for me."

"No problem. You know, you do a pretty good job with your niece. How do you feel about having kids now, Alexis?"

"I would like all that, truthfully, Mom—to be a wife, have a husband."

"You're a beautiful girl, Alexis. Any man would be lucky have you."

"Aww, thanks, Mom. What about you?"

"I'm done. I am not thinking 'bout no man."

I chuckled.

She continued, "You, on the other hand, are still young."

"As soon as we get Santana out of the picture and I get the restaurant up and running, I may consider putting myself out there for love. But right now isn't the time." I thought about James. As much as I liked him, it wouldn't be a good idea to pursue him with Santana running around.

"I'm so tired of that little bastard. I swear, every morning I wake up, I be five seconds from calling him up and offering him money to disappear."

"You think that would work?"

"When in history has it not?"

I shrugged. I guess she was right, but I wasn't so sure. I felt like he had some ulterior motive that I couldn't figure out.

"It's the root of all evil, and that man is evil. If the police can't catch him, I just might take some money and beg his ass to disappear. The only way we are going to be free is with him out of our lives. The other option is killing him, and, well, I don't want to go to prison. So, paying him the money will be the next best option." She looked like she was really contemplating doing this.

"Mom, let the police deal with Santana. We'll be okay. Stay away from him."

But she didn't respond. She just stared off into space and then said, "Let me put the bassinet in your room."

In typical Bria fashion, she did not come in the morning to get the baby, which was fine by me. It gave me the opportunity to spend more time with her. I changed her diaper, gave her a bottle, fed her some baby cereal, gave her a bath, and rubbed her body down with baby lotion until she smelled so good I couldn't stop sniffing and kissing her sweet-looking face. Then I put on a pretty dress and brushed her pretty hair. My mother also had a swing for her, so I took it out to the backyard, put her in it, turned it on, and let her rock in it. She was content and satisfied.

We didn't hear from Bria until five that evening. I was sitting in the kitchen with the baby and my mom, while my mom placed dishes in the dishwasher. I got a call from a blocked number. I assumed it was Bria calling from either her house phone or Casey's cell.

"Hello?" I said quickly.

"You want this to end? You need to meet up with me."

My line clicked, and Bria's number flashed on the screen. I didn't click over, but with a shaking voice, asked instead, "Who is this?"

"Bitch, you know who the fuck this is! Call me back when you're ready, or it is just gonna get worse." My heart was beating fast. I didn't know what to say.

My mother's cell started ringing. "I bet that's Bria. Answer it for me," my mom said.

Before I could think of a response, Santana hung up.

My heart sped up more. It felt like I was having a heart attack. My hands started shaking.

"Mom."

Before she could respond, her phone rang again.

She grabbed her phone quickly off the counter and answered. "So, you still didn't manage to get your baby on time, daughter?"

"Mom," I said.

She looked my way, put a hand up at me, and her eyes narrowed. "Casey?"

All of a sudden, I could hear him howling at the top of his lungs into the phone over and over again, blood-curdling cries.

My mother's eyes narrowed. "Casey, what's going on?"

"Bria!" was all he got out.

My mother's eyes got wide, and she put a hand on her chest. "What's wrong with my child?" she shouted into the phone. "Casey! Casey!"

Casey was now bawling into the phone.

My mom looked at me and said "Alexis, bring the baby!"

My mom grabbed her keys off the wall rack, and I rushed after her with the baby in my arms. I placed the baby in the car seat in the back of my mother's car, and we raced over to Bria's house

Chapter 21

The door was wide open when we arrived, so my mother and I entered the living room. The baby was asleep, so I sat her in the living room while my mother dashed down the hallway. That's when I heard it. My mother was now screaming, much like Casey had been earlier. On shaking legs and with a heart beating so loud I could hear it over my mother's screams, I slowly walked down the hallway in the direction of my mother's screams.

And there was Bria, naked and eyes wide open in a bathtub.

Dead.

There was a hypodermic needle and a vial of heroin on the floor of the bathroom. The belt she had used to tie-off was still wrapped around her arm. It didn't make sense. Why wasn't the needle closer to her body, or still in her arm? Plus, she had never used heroin before. Her drug of choice used to be ecstasy, which Santana had been so kind to get her addicted to. She'd been sober for years, so having a relapse now was strange, because she was happy and didn't want to die. I was certain Bria was dead because someone had killed her. I knew it had to have been Santana. There was no coincidence between the call and this. And that was what I told the officers. The only problem was the number he called me from was blocked, so they merely took my statement. They didn't seem as though they even took it seriously.

Casey's parents arrived as the police were taking my statement. His mother took the baby, who'd woken up, and rocked her. The paramedics had put Bria in a body bag and placed it on a stretcher. As she was wheeled through the living room, Casey collapsed into his father's arms and cried like a baby.

Over and over again, he said, "My baby gone! My baby gone! Why? Why?"

And yes, tears continued to stream down my face, and a hurt feeling crushed my chest. My sister was gone. Just as we were mending our relationship, she was taken from me. First my dad, and now her. It hurt more than I thought it would. I couldn't wrap my head around the fact that she was no longer on this earth. Her life was taken from her before she got the chance to fully live it, and she didn't deserve that. She had a beautiful little girl that would grow up without her, a husband who was now a widower, a mom who was down one of her kids, and me. It hurt because we had finally gotten to a good place, and I was looking forward to more time and memories with her.

I covered my face with both of my hands, and my body was wracked with sobs. I would have preferred to have been taken instead of her. For the first time in a long time, I wished they had never let me out of prison. Then maybe, just maybe, life for my family would have stayed the same, just without me really in it. If I had stayed away, Santana would probably not have come back around. I hated myself. And the way my mother couldn't look at me, the way Casey's eyes continued to shoot my way, I knew they hated me too.

Two weeks later, we buried my sister. How could I sum it up? To sit in the service and feel like you're responsible for the death . . . to feel like you should and would gladly take the spot in the casket. So many moments, I prayed to God to reverse this, to take me, but I knew I was being stupid, impractical, and illogical, because what was done was done. It could not be erased or changed.

I couldn't really listen to the sermon, because I continued to be haunted by Bria's voice, or the cute way she smiled and laughed, or her wacky personality. Her free spirit was something I always admired but never admitted to her. No matter what, she always knew how to have fun, and she had this natural spunk about her. Trying to focus on what was going on in front of me wasn't much better. As I looked around the church, I noticed how much her little girl favored her as she sat on Casey's mother's lap, totally oblivious to what was going on around her or the fact that her mother was gone. This did nothing but bring forth the reality that she would never be held, kissed, or in the presence of her again. Then I looked at the pain on Casey's face and the rage on my mother's. Since we discovered my sister's body, my mom still had not looked at me.

I stared down at the picture of my sister on the obituary. She was smiling with Nya in her arms. I don't think there was a picture of her ever looking so pretty or even happier. I looked up and listened to the few who chose to stand up and say something about Bria. This now had me with my head in my right shoulder, hiding my face as tears soaked the top side of my dress. My throat just felt so scratchy. The part I was dreading the most was my obligation to the funeral.

I had been asked to sing. The song I was supposed to sing was called "Forever with Me" by Yolanda Adams. It was my sister's favorite song. I got up calmly and walked to the stage. I grabbed the mic and closed my eyes briefly as more emotion hit me.

Someone said, "That's all right, baby."

I opened my eyes, closed them again, and gritted my teeth as the music started. But I wasn't ready, so the band stopped. I took two more breaths and nodded, letting the band know that I was now ready.

"Looking over the horizon, night breaks into dawn. I get a little misty-eyed, knowing you're gone."

My mother instantly broke into tears. Her tears caused tears of my own to where the next words, I just couldn't get them out.

"I–I—" My voice cracked. "I'm so sorry," I said. I was unable to even finish the song because my voice continued to crack. The choir chimed in while I took a deep breath.

I heard from someone, "It's okay, Alexis. Take your time, baby."

I wiped my tears, took another deep breath, and sang the song the best I could. I pretended my sister was standing in front of me, clapping and cheering me on. I thought of the last time I saw her, when we were dancing together. That was the only way I was able to finish, by thinking of a good moment between her and me. I couldn't not finish, because this was the day I had to say goodbye to her, whether I wanted to or not. And damned if I wanted to.

Again, I thought, *We were just getting started.*

I finished with the line, "I love you. I'm gonna miss you. You're forever here with me." I then sat back down and looked at her casket again. I saw the swell of her hands resting across her chest. This caused the tears to flow again.

I prayed in my head that the service would end, and I watched as people went to her casket. Arianna sat down next to me and wrapped an arm around me.

"It's okay, Alexis."

I sobbed on her left shoulder. All I could think about was how much time my sister and I had wasted being petty. It seemed like that went on forever. And then we put our differences aside and got close. That was short lived. See, it wasn't just the hurt of losing Bria; it was the fact that I unequivocally blamed myself.

"Alexis, do you want to go up to her casket?"

I shook my head. "I don't think I can, Arianna," I said between sobs.

"I love you, Alexis, and yes, you can say goodbye to your sister. Would it help if I go up there with you?"

I nodded my head. "Yes, please."

Arianna helped me to my feet, and we slowly walked up to the casket. I leaned over and looked at her pretty face. She didn't look dead. She looked like she was resting peacefully, but I knew her last moments had to be anything but peaceful.

I leaned my face down to kiss one of her cheeks. The cold feeling had me teared up again. I rested my face on her chest and sobbed.

That's when I heard, "Get off of her!"

It was Casey. With a hateful expression, he grabbed me by the back of my hair, causing Arianna to scream. He threw me so hard I flew into one of the pews.

"Casey, no!!" his mother yelled. "Stop!"

His dad stood up and restrained him. My mom weakly cried from the pew and covered her face with both her hands.

I looked up at the hateful look in his eyes.

"No! She is the reason why Bria is gone. She is the one who was screwing her brother. She brought this into Bria's world, and now she is gone because of her!"

I nodded my head. He was right. It was because of me. I felt it, and I felt it again. I wished I had never been released from prison. And as he spat what he spat, the members of our church, who had appeared to have forgiven me, now seemed like they felt the same way Casey felt. But the thing was, it didn't matter if they did or didn't, because deep down, it was the way that I felt.

I stood to my feet and ran out of the church, down the stairs, and down the street. I could hear my name being called.

"Alexis! Stop, Alexis!"

Arianna and Justin both ran after me. They were able to catch me at the corner of the church. No words were said. They simply both just hugged me. And yes, it felt good for them to do it.

And yet, as Casey's words came back in my head I said, "I deserved everything he said. Every word, every hate eye." I pulled away from them and placed my hands at my temples as they throbbed, and I said in a weak voice, "This is really my fault. My fucked-up decisions landed us where we are now."

"Alexis!" Arianna said. "You have to stop doing this to yourself! You did not do this! You have come too far to go back now."

Gently, Justin said, "She is right, Alexis. What Casey said and what Casey did . . . It was wrong. And even though this may sound crazy, it had nothing to do with you."

I shook my head.

"Alexis, I wish there was some way to get you to see the truth. And the truth is that what you just saw was his pain. That's all that was. He is hurting because he lost his wife, and he lashed out at the person that was a really super target. What he is going through has to be extremely difficult. I mean, he lost his wife. But that doesn't make it right, what he said, or putting his hands on you. I'd bet you half of that church doesn't even know what he really is thinking and *who* he really blames. But I'ma shut up on that.

"You're a smart girl. You should know things aren't always what they seem. Read between the lines. You also really can't take what the church says seriously either. He is their pastor and in pain, and often, whether he is wrong or right, they are going to roll with him. But never forget, Casey was a man that never really respected his wife or the sanctity of his marriage. So, he openly, in the church's face, was disobeying God. Still, they won't see it, and even if they do, they will turn a blind eye to it. So sexist. But, Alexis, understand those are inner issues he's got going on, and he deflected in front of the church, making a fool of himself."

Justin hugged me tighter and said, "I won't tell you to cheer up, but I will say give your mind some ease and allow yourself to grieve . . . in peace, my friend."

Chapter 22

The repast was at our house. I went upstairs to my room to be away from everyone who attended. My embarrassment and guilt prevented me from being social. I watched out my bedroom window as the guests arrived. I wondered if the situation at the church had kept some of the parishioners away. It was all my fault. My sister was probably not getting the proper send-off she deserved, because I was the cause of drama at her funeral.

I lay on my bed and sighed. My past mistakes were haunting me and had resulted in the death of my sister, blocking me from any sort of real reconciliation with her. Santana had to be stopped.

Tears rolled down my cheeks as I thought about my sister. It hurt me that her daughter would never know her mother. I was feeling sorry for myself, but I thought about Justin's words, and they made me feel a little better. Only a little. He came to check on me and tried to cheer me up. He danced for me, he hugged me, and gave me words of encouragement, but nothing was going to fully get me out of my funk.

My mother hadn't come up to say anything to me. Usually, she would have had me come downstairs when there were people visiting, but that day, she stayed away.

It was evident to me that she was blaming me for Bria's death. I didn't blame her; she was right.

Soon after Justin left, there was a knock on my door.

"Come in," I said.

Casey's mother opened the door and poked her head in. "Somebody's looking for you." She was holding Nya.

I chuckled, stood, and put sanitizer on my hands quickly before taking the baby in my arms.

"Little Miss Busybody is not trying to go to sleep. She was looking around, being nosy."

I chuckled and sat back down with Nya in my arms. I stared down at her pretty face as she looked at me with wide eyes.

"Alexis, I'm sorry for what my—" She cleared her throat. "For how my son treated you."

"It's okay. He is in pain. I understand."

"It's not okay. You are in pain too."

I offered the best smile I could, which I knew was probably tight.

"Well, I'm gonna go downstairs."

When she reached for Nya, I said, "Can she stay with me for a little while?"

"Of course. I just changed her, so she should be okay." She leaned over and kissed me on the cheek. I appreciated her coming to check on me. She slipped out of the room and gently closed the door behind her.

That gave me time to engage with little Nya. She was now able to hold her head up, and when I cooed, her little face burst into the biggest smile.

"Awww." My eyes got a little watery. "Such a pretty girl."

Then, out of nowhere, her bottom lip poked out and started trembling.

"Oh, no," I said in a soft voice. "Not the lip." I poked my lip out too, and she pulled her lip back in and started laughing.

"You tricked me!"

She burst into another smile.

I pulled her closer to me and kissed her on her neck repeatedly, causing her to make a cooing sound. I was so glad to be able to interact with the baby. Her innocence took some of the hurt away. I couldn't be sad looking at such a hopeful beauty. Seeing her little face and knowing my sister lived on through her felt good. Nya would carry on my sister's legacy. I prayed Casey wouldn't hate me forever, because I really wanted to be in Nya's life and watch her mature into a responsible woman.

Nya started rubbing her eyes, a tell-tale sign she was sleepy. I began rocking her. Within a couple minutes, she was knocked out. I continued to hold her in my arms. I was sure there was nothing better than having a sleeping baby curled up in my arms. I laid her down on the bed and curled up next to her. Watching her little chest rise up and down, I knew I had to be in her life. I knew it would probably be better to lay low, and hopefully Casey would come around and let me.

There was another knock on my door.

"Who is it?" I said softly.

After a pregnant pause, I heard, "Casey."

I took a sharp intake of breath. I prepared for him to come in and unleash on me, perhaps even get physical. Then remembered I did have his daughter in my room, and he was probably coming to collect her. I just hoped he didn't snap on me again.

I said, "Come in."

He came in and closed the door behind him. I didn't like that. I would have been more comfortable with the door open. Assuming he was there to get the baby and to get him out of there as quick as possible, I reached for her and said, "She fell asleep."

"No, it's fine. I ummm—" He cleared his face, looked away, then looked back at me and said, "I came to talk to you."

I looked at him, surprised, and nodded.

"Look. I'm really sorry, Alexis. My lashing out the way I did. It doesn't take anyone to tell me that it was wrong. I knew I was wrong when I did it." He leaned back against the door and banged his head backward, hitting the back of his head lightly.

"I never blamed you. I couldn't. Because this—" His shoulders shuddered and tears started falling. "Lord, this is so hard. No one knows this." He slid down to the floor. "I'm responsible for Bria dying."

"No, you're not."

"Listen. I lied to her. Told her I was going to the church. But I—" He started breathing, and that turned to sobbing so hard his whole body shook. "I left my wife in her last moments to fuck another woman!"

I gasped.

"In her last moments, when she needed me the most, I was fucking another woman." He punched himself in the chest with both hands. "I did this, Alexis. Not you." His lips trembled, and he locked eyes with me. "She asked me not to go. Said she wanted us to stay in bed. Asked me to order us some breakfast and we stay in bed. Said you wouldn't trip. But I made it seem like I had so much to do, and I didn't."

"Casey."

He held up a hand. "No, don't console me. I don't deserve it. My wife kept her promise to me and stopped sleeping around, but I never did. I failed her. I killed her." He leaned forward and lay on the floor on his stomach and cried like a baby in his forearms. "Dear God, I didn't protect my baby. My wife."

I stood from the bed walked over to him and kneeled down and tried to hug him.

"I don't deserve comfort. I don't deserve it. I want to die. I don't deserve it."

But even as he said this, I continued to comfort him by hugging him. "You didn't kill her."

As he cried miserably on my floor and I continued to hug him as best I could and provide him with more comforting words, I couldn't help but look at little Nya still sleeping peacefully on the bed. In that moment, I knew what was important—stopping Santana any way I could so Nya could grow up in a world without the chaos of Santana. All I knew and felt was that since I was the one who did this, I would have to be the one to fix it. End it.

Chapter 23

The next week was torture. I was depressed and couldn't stop thinking about Bria. Everything reminded me of her. The food I ate, the television shows I watched, the places I drove . . . it didn't matter what, I was thinking of Bria.

I didn't see my mother at all. She would get up early in the morning and be out of the house until late at night. I wasn't sure if she was purposely trying to avoid me, but it sure seemed that way. We were like two roommates who never got together. I desperately wanted to speak to her. I needed her at that time to comfort me.

Hoping to smooth things over, I called my mother. Her phone went to voicemail.

"Hi, Mom. I am going to see Nya and was wondering if you wanted to come with. Casey said you could come too, so just come over if you want." I ended the call and hoped my mother would show up so we could talk about Bria. I needed her to forgive me.

Casey was waiting for me when I showed up to his house. I could feel Bria's energy as I walked in, or maybe I thought I felt her energy because I could smell her perfume. Whatever it was, Bria was still a force in that house.

Casey looked tired. He had bags under his eyes. It looked like he hadn't shaved in a week, and he was wearing pajamas at three o'clock in the afternoon. My heart went out to him. He closed the door behind me. I hugged him, and he squeezed me tight and cried on my shoulder. Feeling his sobbing penetrated my soul, and I cried along with him. We stood locked in that embrace for a few minutes, each of us absorbing the other's pain and releasing it into the universe. When we were able to compose ourselves, we released each other.

He wiped the tears from his face. "Sorry. I've been holding that in. When I saw you, I couldn't control it," he said.

"I understand. Don't be sorry. I needed to release my sadness."

"This isn't easy."

"It will never be easy. The pain and sadness will be less, but it will never go away."

Nya cooed from her bassinet. "She's the only thing keeping me sane. If it wasn't for my baby, I don't know if I could go on."

"Casey, you will get through this. I will be here for you. Whenever you need to talk, or whatever you need, I'll be here for you."

"Thanks, Alexis. That means a lot."

"Now, go get yourself cleaned up. Take a shower, shave, and put some real clothes on. I'll watch Nya."

"Yeah, you're right. I need to break out of this. A shower will feel good."

Casey went upstairs. I heard the shower turn on. I took Nya out of her bassinet and hugged her. I laid a blanket on the floor and put her in the middle on her back. She was so beautiful. She had changed so much in the week since I'd seen her at the funeral. She was more alert and beginning to look even more like Bria. When I sang to her, she stared at me. I looked into her eyes and could see her absorbing the music. Her brain was working overtime and processing and storing everything. I was blessed to have the time with her. I wanted her to remember me and know how much I loved her.

As I was feeding her a bottle of formula and rocking her to sleep, Casey came downstairs. He looked like a new man. He was clean shaven and had on a tight Calvin Klein V-neck sweater and dark Calvin Klein blue jeans. I must say he was looking fine. I could see why Bria was so head over heels for him. Though, if he was my man, I wouldn't have cheated on him like she did. Oh well, I guess that was the nature of their relationship. They were both cheaters who were crazy about each other.

"How do you feel?" I whispered so as not to disturb Nya.

"I needed that. Thanks." He rubbed his cheek and chin where his scraggly beard used to be. He sat down on the couch across from me and Nya.

We looked at each other. Even though he was cleaned up, I could still see the hurt in his eyes. I needed to do whatever I could to blunt that hurt for all of us—me, my mother, and Casey. The only way we would be able to move on would be for me to kill Santana. It was risky, and I could potentially go back to prison, but it would be worth it, and I'd gladly spend the rest of my life behind bars if it meant Santana wouldn't be able to torture any of us ever again.

"I can't believe she's gone," Casey said.

"I know. It doesn't seem real."

He looked at Nya sleeping in my arms. "What am I going to tell her when she asks about her mother?"

"The truth. That she was a kind, beautiful, loving mother. Tell her she had a disease that she bravely fought, but in the end, the disease won."

"Thanks, Alexis."

I looked down at Nya. She looked so peaceful in her sleep. I wondered what she was dreaming about. I prayed that all of her dreams would come true.

"Casey," I said, "I have to say that I feel responsible for Bria's death, but I'm going to make it right."

"What do you mean? It wasn't your fault."

"It was. Her death has Santana written all over it. If I had never gotten involved with him, this wouldn't have happened. It's time that I put an end to his terror."

"Alexis, don't talk stupid. Let the authorities handle Santana. Nya is going to need her auntie in her life. Don't go doing anything that could jeopardize that."

"I won't. I love little Nya and will never do anything to harm her or upset her."

"Good. This is nice having someone to talk to about everything. Can we make this a habit? I'd like for you to be in Nya's life as much as possible. She's going to need a female around to emulate and learn from."

"I would love that. I'm honored." My eyes teared up.

"Here, let me put her in her bassinet." Casey took Nya from me.

We both stood over her bassinet for a few seconds, watching her little chest going up and down.

"I should get going," I said.

"Okay, be safe, Alexis."

We held each other tight in our goodbye hug. It felt good to be in the tight embrace of a man. I inhaled his scent as my face buried in his muscular chest. He kissed the top of my head and released me. I wasn't ready to let go, but I did. In that moment, I thought about James. I needed to see him.

I left the house in a state of arousal. Feeling Casey's body against mine had me feeling some sort of way. I wasn't about to do anything with my sister's husband, but damn if I didn't think about it for a second.

Chapter 24

I needed to feel James's naked body next to mine. I called him as I left Casey's home. I could feel butterflies in my stomach as I waited for him to answer. With the way I left it the last time I saw him, there was no guarantee he would answer. He could have moved on for all I knew. I had told him I had to stay away from him, so I couldn't expect a man to not date other women, especially a man as fine as James.

Just as I was preparing for his phone to go to voice-mail, he answered.

"Alexis?" he said.

"Hi."

"I wasn't expecting to hear from you. Is everything all right?"

"I'm good. I just wanted to say hi and see how you're doing."

"I'm better. Not fully healed. Who knew recovering from a gunshot took so long?" He laughed.

Neither of us said anything after that. I could hear him breathing on the other end.

He finally broke the silence. "So, you wanna come over? You know, since I got shot because of you."

"That's not funny, James."

"I'm sorry. I'm just trying to lighten the mood. But I'd love to see you."

"You sure you want to see me?"

"Yes, I'm sure."

"I'd like that. I'll come over now."

James greeted me at his door wearing a grey zip-up hooded sweatshirt and jeans. It was nice to see him up and out of the hospital. He looked like he had made a full recovery. His skin was glowing, and I could make out his tight body underneath his tight clothing. I admit, I looked for the bulge in his jeans.

He stepped aside and let me enter, then closed the door behind me. We faced each other, and he took my hand in his.

"It's nice to see you," he said.

"Yeah, you too. You look much better than the last time we saw each other."

"I'm feeling stronger every day. I've started to get back in the gym."

"I can tell." I squeezed his bicep with my free hand.

The touch led to a hug, which led to a kiss. The next thing I knew, we were in his bedroom, making love. It felt so good to have his masculine frame cover my body as I opened my legs for him. He stroked me so good my insides were burning with desire. He had me cumming multiple times.

Hours later, we lay in his bed. He had his arm around me, and my head rested on his shoulder while I gently rubbed his bullet wound.

"I'm sorry I got you shot," I said.

"It's not your fault. I'd take a bullet for you any day."

"Because of me, Santana is terrorizing everyone I love."

"He is too reckless. He'll get caught. Just give it time." James kissed the top of my head.

"Time is running out. He killed my sister; he almost killed you. He won't stop until we are all dead. I can't have that. He's out of control, and the police don't seem to take it seriously."

"What are you saying?"

"I'm going to take matters into my own hands. He needs to be stopped."

"Alexis, he is dangerous. You know that."

"I've thought about it a lot. Too much, in fact. It's the only way."

"I want to help you. You can't do it alone, and I can't take losing you. I've been down since you've stayed away, and I don't want that feeling anymore. I need you."

I looked into his eyes and saw his passion. I felt the same way. We kissed, our tongues exploring each other's mouths.

He pulled away from me. "So, Santana is hurting everyone you love. Does that mean you love me?" He smiled.

I took a moment before I answered. "Let's say I like you very much, and I love how you fuck me."

"Good enough for me," James said, then he flipped me on my back and fucked me again.

Chapter 25

The next morning, I woke up completely satisfied in James's bed. I hadn't had a sex-filled night like the previous night in a long time. I smiled as I stretched in his king-size bed, luxuriating in his soft sheets and warm comforter. It felt like a five-star hotel bed. I turned to snuggle into James, and he wasn't there.

I got out of bed and looked through his dresser for a T-shirt to put on. I found one in his top drawer, a black shirt with *Howard University* printed across the front. I put it on, and it hung down just below my ass.

I went downstairs to look for James. I found him in the kitchen reading the newspaper.

"I thought I'd find you in here. Was hoping there would be breakfast waiting for me," I said.

"I didn't want to subject you to my cooking. It's not very good. I thought I'd take you out to eat."

"That's a nice thought, but how about I whip something up here? I'm opening my restaurant soon and need as much practice in the kitchen as possible. Besides, I'd rather have my attention on you, not some restaurant filled with people."

"You won't catch me complaining about that." He grabbed me around my waist and pulled me into him. We kissed. I was glad I'd rinsed my mouth with mouthwash before coming downstairs.

James didn't have much food to work with, but I was able to make us French toast, eggs, and sausage. Nothing fancy, but I did the best I could with the ingredients I was given.

James took a bite of French toast. "If this is a sample of what your restaurant is serving, I'm going to be there every day."

I laughed.

"I'm serious. This is possibly the best French toast I've ever had."

"Well, thank you. It's hard to screw up French toast, though."

"You'd think differently about that if you'd ever had my sorry excuse for French toast."

"You keep layin' it down in the bedroom like you do, and your cooking won't matter."

He raised his eyebrows. "Really? I think I can manage that, especially with a beautiful woman such as yourself."

We quickly finished breakfast and immediately went back to his bedroom. I was like a giddy teenager with James. I craved his body and would do anything to please him. We spent the rest of the morning in bed, exploring each other's bodies. By the time we finished, James's tongue had been over every inch of me.

James stroked my hair. "So, tell me about your restaurant."

"Well, it's almost finished. It won't be anything fancy, just a casual place with great food and great service. I want it to be a place that feels like home to people."

"I can't wait to see it."

"I have to go over there today. Come with me."

"I would like that."

We showered together then got ready to leave. James let me wash my clothes before we left. I appreciated that he understood I didn't feel like wearing the same dirty clothes I wore the day before. While we waited for my clothes, we curled up on the couch and watched some reality TV. I hated the way the shows depicted women of color. At that point in my life, I wanted to see more uplifting portrayals of African Americans.

When my clothes were finished, we drove to the restaurant. I was nervous as I opened the door for James. No one had seen the place yet except me and my workers. His reaction would be a test for my vision of the restaurant.

James stepped through the door, walked in a few steps, and stopped. He took in the surroundings. I watched and waited in anticipation of his reaction.

I couldn't stand the silence. I had to say something. "It's not finished yet, but with the right lighting and music, you'll really get a feel for it."

"Alexis, I think the place looks amazing already. Lighting and music will make this place the hottest new restaurant, for sure."

I smiled.

"I'm serious. I'm so proud of you."

"Let me show you the kitchen. I'll cook you something off the menu."

I cooked him grilled chicken with sweet potatoes and asparagus in a sunflower butter sauce. I had him sit in the restaurant and served him like he was a paying customer. After he tasted the first bite and loved it, I relaxed and sat with him. He devoured the food. It was so nice to see him enjoy my cooking. It gave me confidence that my restaurant would be successful. I couldn't wait to open it to the public.

James had a few things to take care of after he ate, so he went on his way. I stayed back and cleaned up the kitchen with a smile on my face the entire time. With James, it felt that my life was taking a turn for the best.

I locked up the restaurant and drove home. On my way, I received a text: **Looks like you had a day and night with your fuck boi. Shoulda killed him when I had the chance.**

My heart sank. Had Santana been following us? It freaked me out that he could be so close to see what I was doing, yet I had no idea he was there. I stopped at a red light and looked in every direction. I didn't see him anywhere. The rest of the ride home, I was checking my rearview for Santana. I was paranoid he would drive up and shoot at me again.

I got home, and my hands were shaking as I unlocked the front door. This game of his needed to end.

Chapter 26

I went up to my room and responded to the text. I told Santana he could meet me at the restaurant the next day. I was going to put an end to this once and for all. I wished I could give the number to the police and let them handle it, but Santana always contacted me from different numbers, so I assumed he used burner phones, which couldn't be traced back to him. He was crazy, not stupid.

At the end of the day, I didn't at all know what it was that Santana really wanted or how I could fix this and make this right. I wasn't sure reasoning with him would make a difference. Negotiating with him might work, but what did he really want, and what could I give in return? Whatever I had to do, I sure was going to try, because the thing was, there were only two other people he could hurt: my mother or Nya. And because of how sick and foul he was, I wouldn't put it past him.

The next day, I showed up a half hour earlier than I had told him. I unlocked the place and waited on him to arrive. I paced the restaurant. This showdown was long overdue. I was scared. Not for me—I mean, he had already done the worst to me when he had me locked up, killed my sister, and shot my boyfriend. Did I think James was my boyfriend? I realized I wanted him to be my boyfriend. Thinking about the extreme lengths

Santana would go to, I was scared for what might happen if I was unable to stop him.

As the minutes flew by, I kept looking out the window for him. There were dark storm clouds slowly moving in. It was a bad omen in my opinion. I walked to the back of the restaurant to check the back door. As I pulled the locked door, I heard the front door open.

My heart sped up as I anticipated his appearance. I quietly walked toward the front, attempting to stay out of sight so I could assess the situation before confronting Santana. Only it wasn't Santana. It was my mother, carrying a duffel bag.

I looked down at my phone and saw there was still a good ten minutes until Santana would be there. I had to get my mother out of there. There was no telling what would happen once Santana showed up.

I rushed up to her. She looked at me, surprised, and we both said in unison, "What are you doing here?"

I shook my head. "Mom, I don't have time to explain." I turned her around and said, "You have to get out of here."

She pulled away from me and said, "No! You need to leave!" She grabbed me and shoved me towards the door.

"What are you doing?"

"Just do what I'm asking you to do!"

I yanked away from her in tears from panic over her being there, and tears from how cruel she was treating me. "I know you hate me, Mom. I'm sure you blame me for Bria's death. I blame myself too. But you have to—" A sob wracked my body.

"This is not about you! Santana's coming! All right? That's why I don't want you here."

My stomach flip-flopped, and my heart started beating sharply. How did she know he was coming?

"I know, and I need to deal with him," I said. "Alone."

She strong-armed me and hooked one of her arms around my neck and propelled me forward with all her might. I dug my feet into the floor, but still, my mother managed to pull me forward.

"Mom, stop! You don't know what you're doing!"

"Shut up!"

I struggled back against her as she gripped her arm tighter on my neck. When she reached to open the door, I kicked it closed. I wasn't going to leave her there with Santana. He was getting more violent in his actions, and I wanted to get her out of there, period.

My mom slapped me in my face with her free hand, hitting me in my left eye. I closed my eyes and winced at the pain. She took the diversion to open the door again.

The door flew open, and Santana stood there at the entrance. My mom released me, and I fell to the floor. My mom backed up, and I scrambled back to my feet.

"Just the two bitches I came to see," he said.

"No. My daughter is leaving."

"Mom, no! You need to leave!"

"How about both of y'all bird-brain bitches both shut the fuck up!" He closed the door and stepped farther into the room.

"Now, none of y'all is leaving, because I set this off for both of y'all to be here."

My mom shook her head. "Santana," she said evenly, "I would like—"

"Did you hear what I just said? Now, I don't give a fuck what you would like. I want the both of you here!"

My mom closed her eyes, and her body shuddered. "Don't hurt my daughter."

"Shut the hell up. I told both of y'all. This can end very easily. Today."

"Okay." My mom shook her head.

Santana stared at me maliciously. "Go on and sit the fuck down, Alexis."

My mother and I slid into a booth. Santana sat across from us. He stared at us both with a sinister expression on his face.

"You killed my daughter," my mom said.

He chuckled. "Little Bria. Hey, I heard that was an overdose. She was still fucking with that shit?" Then he burst into hard laughter. My mother looked away. "My bad. I'm sorry for your loss." He chuckled.

"Listen, I want this to end. I want this to be over. I have close to a million dollars. Seven hundred thousand, to be exact," my mother said.

His eyes widened.

"It's in this duffle bag." She motioned to the bag in her lap. "If I give it to you, I would like for you to leave California. Never come back or contact me or my daughter again, got it?"

"No."

My mom looked at him, surprised.

"I don't want the money. I want you, Mom."

"Well, I can't ever, ever give you that, not after all you've done. Now, do you want money?"

His nostrils flared as his fists hit the table. "I just told you I don't want the fucking money!"

"What do you expect, Santana? I made a choice long ago. I did not want you. And now, after all that you have done, even if I had changed my mind and wanted a relationship, it could never be possible. You got my daughter locked up! You killed my baby!"

His expression relaxed, and for once he looked remorseful. "Maybe my actions were wrong what I did to Alexis, her sister, your husband, and the pain I purposely caused you. But they are good. Alexis is out of prison, Bria is—"

"Was," I corrected him.

"Okay. She was married to a pastor and had a kid. Listen, I don't know whether you believe me or not, but I had no intention to kill her. I just wanted to get her hooked on the drug. Whether you believe it or not all these things I've done were just temper tantrums. Ways to cry out for your attention. Don't you get it, Mom? I just want you in my life. And I'm sorry for all the things I've done. That alone grants me a second chance to have you in my life as a mom."

He may not have had the intentions for things to go the way they went, but they did, so that made him responsible. He was really a psychopath. He killed my sister and really thought my mother could forgive that. Could forgive him.

"Will you at least give it some thought?"

"No. I am willing to give you the money. Then we can go our separate ways."

He quickly reached across the table and enclosed his hand around my neck. My mom stood and placed a hand over his, trying to loosen his grip. He pulled out a gun with his other hand, pointed it at my mother, and said, "Sit the fuck down."

My mom did so quickly. "Please stop hurting her," she begged.

He gripped my necked harder and choked me until I couldn't breathe and snot flew from my nose. I tried to fight back, but the lack of oxygen was sapping my strength. The entire time, he stared at my mother. Just as I was about to pass out, he released me.

I grabbed my neck and started coughing.

"You promised no guns if I promised no police," I said.

"Well, bitch, I lied."

He slid from the booth and rushed up to my mom, pausing in front of her. "Bitch, I hate you! Get up!" He snatched my mom by her shirt, until she was on her feet, and yanked her out of the booth. He then put the gun to her left temple, causing me to fly from the booth, flailing my arms.

I began begging him, "Please, don't shoot her!"

Then he removed it, backed up, and placed it at his own temple. I prayed he would pull the trigger.

"Rejected at birth and rejected as an adult." He turned his attention to me. "Alexis, you need not protect this bitch. If you only knew just how foul she was and still is, just by the fact that she gave up her first born! Alexis, do you know the real story about your holy-roller, sanctified mother and how I was born?"

He stalked up to me and pointed the gun in my face. "Answer me, dingbat, 'cause I'm tired."

"Y–yes," I said in a shaky voice.

"Then tell me."

"She was sleeping with her dad's business partner. She got pregnant and found out he was also sleeping with her mom. So. So—"

"So! Come on, mothafucka, keep going."

"So, her father killed the business partner and her mother."

His head snapped back, and his eyes were wide. "You lying, trifling bitch!" He swung the gun in the air violently.

"That ain't what the fuck happened. But, Alexis, I'ma tell you what happened. Yes, the hot-in-the-panties bitch was scheming and fucking her dad's business partner. My dad. And yes, he was fucking her mother, who wasn't nothing but a trifling ho like her. But her daddy ain't kill no one." He gestured at her mother with the gun. "This bitch did."

I gasped.

"Her mother and my father were going to run away together, and your mom wasn't going for that shit. So, this bitch, she killed her mother on the night she was set to run away with my dad. Shot her with her father's gun.

"And her dad, he was a pussy. Couldn't bear the thought of his precious daughter going to prison. He did, after all, blame himself for not knowing my dad was fucking his wife and daughter right under his nose. So, he took the blame. Killed himself not even a year later while locked up, which got this tramp off when she deserved to rot in prison. Or hell."

I looked at my mom as she put her head down in shame. She didn't deny it, so I knew it had to be true.

My mom was now crying and shaking. "No more, please."

His lips curled into a snarl. "No more? Mama, I'm getting to the best part. Alexis, did your mom tell you that we have more in common than just her?"

I looked away. I didn't want to hear what he was about to say.

"Yeah. That business partner, he never went away. Yes, the bitch gave me up. And when the coast was clear, she relocated to California. But she never stopped sneaking away to fuck my daddy. I guess he had some good dick. And just for your information, the only kid her dumb-ass husband fathered was Bria. You and I have the same father."

He whipped his head around and glared at my mom. "Didn't think I knew, huh, Mom? I was lucky enough to find him before he passed, and he led me right to you. He wasn't shit, and neither were you! But at least he didn't willingly get you pregnant again after you gave your first born away. That choice was yours!"

My eyes widened as my mother moaned. As I reeled from what he said about my mother and father, Santana got close to my mother and spit in her face.

My mom shuddered.

"Bitch, all my life I wanted and cried for you. You never stopped sleeping with my dad but still never wanted me! Still never came back to get me! You were okay with him not wanting me, and you still wanted him." He pointed at me. "And I hated this bitch because she took my place. I just couldn't get how you could keep her and not me. I was thrown away because of the unfortunate event you caused. So, to not relive it, you just got rid of me. Mom, I hate you too." He stuck the gun in my mother's face.

He shook his head and said, "Even with a gun in your face, you mean to tell me that you still think you are going to get away a second time for abandoning me? Bitch, you gonna die first!"

Just as he was about to pull the trigger, the front door opened. "Alexis—"

Santana whipped around and wildly fired a shot at James, who ducked to avoid the bullet. The bullet was off target and lodged into the wall behind James. I took the opportunity to rush Santana and jump on his back. He easily flung me off, turned back around, punched my mother in her face, knocking her out, and fired a shot at me. The bullet hit me in my lower back. I was dropped to the floor immediately.

James took advantage of the distraction and tackled Santana. The two men wrestled. James was struggling to knock the gun out of Santana's hand. I was stunned and bleeding.

The gun got dislodged from Santana's hand. I attempted to crawl to it, but I couldn't. My legs were not moving. I tried with all my might to move, but I couldn't. The exertion was making me weak. I was on my way to blacking out; I could feel it.

Just before I passed out, Santana punched James and was able to get up and go for his gun. I closed my eyes.

The last thing I heard was, "Police! Drop your weapon."

I woke up in a hospital bed, connected to a bunch of machines. It was night, but what time, what day? I found the call button for the nurse and pushed it. I tried to sit up while I waited for the nurse, but I was too weak. I couldn't feel my legs.

The nurse came in a hurry. "You're awake," she said.

"Where am I? What happened?" I asked.

"You're in the intensive care unit. You were brought here two days ago, in bad shape. You had lost a lot of blood from a gunshot wound. I'll have the doctor come in and explain everything." She checked a few of the machines. "Do you need anything?"

"Some water would be nice."

"I'll get that for you. There are a few people who will be very happy to know you are awake. I'll let them know as well." She left the room.

As I lay there, I realized something felt different. I looked down at my legs and tried to bend my knees. Nothing happened. I reached down to move them with my hands. When I grabbed my right thigh, I couldn't feel my hands on it. I panicked, and the heart monitor started beeping faster. I grabbed my left thigh, and the same thing happened. I had no feeling in either leg, and they wouldn't move when I tried to bend them.

As I was reaching down to try to touch my toes, James walked in.

He smiled. "Alexis."

"James, I can't move my legs. What happened?"

He came to my bedside. "Santana shot you in the back. The bullet was lodged in your spine. The doctors were able to get it out, but—" He looked down at the floor.

"But what? Tell me, James. But what?"

"There was damage to the nerves to your legs. You are paralyzed from the waist down. I'm so sorry, Alexis."

I didn't know what to say or do. I looked at James, and tears silently fell down my cheeks. He leaned over and hugged me. I cried in his shoulder.

"I'll be here to help you and do whatever needs to be done. I'm not going anywhere. I want to be your rock."

As we broke our hug, my mother, Arianna, and Casey walked in. My mother was already crying. She came over and wrapped her arms around me.

"My baby," she said.

"What happened?" I asked.

My mother wiped the tears from her eyes. "Santana had gotten both of us to show up at your restaurant. He was going to kill us, for sure. Luckily, I had called the police to tip them off that Santana would be there."

James said, "Yeah, I happened to drive by and saw your car, so I stopped in to see you. When I went in, he shot at me. We wrestled, and the cops showed up. Santana didn't listen when they told him to drop the weapon. He committed suicide by cop. They laid him out quick."

No one said anything for a few seconds. I broke the silence. "So, Santana is dead?"

James nodded his head.

My mother said "Yes, baby."

I looked at everyone standing around my bed—the most important people in my life. I was so lucky to have such loving friends and family. My redemption was complete.

I began laughing. "We are finally rid of him."